THE LAST WITNESS

THE LAST WITNESS

G V SUBBA RAO

Vitasta

Published by
Renu Kaul Verma
Vitasta Publishing Pvt Ltd
4348/4C, Ansari Road, Daryaganj
New Delhi - 110 002
info@vitastapublishing.com

ISBN: 978-81-19670-12-3

First Edition 2024
MRP ₹350

Edited by Soumitro Das and Reena Singh
Typeset by Rohit Gautam
Cover Design by Somesh Kumar Mishra
Printed at Chaman Enterprises, New Delhi

To my mother, Smt Sundari Gollapudi, w/o Shri Gollapudi Maruthi Rao, who nurtured and raised me and then left me on 28/01/2022.

I look up to the stars at night searching for you in the vast continuum. The story, 'The Last Witness' emerged from the dark corners of my mind, and I still feel your presence here and now.

1

Indian Space Research Organisation, Sriharikota

Dr Rangarajan, preferred a stroll rather than taking the official car. The renowned ISRO (Indian Space Research Organisation) scientist, who was in his late fifties, stepped out thoughtfully from his office to go home, that was a couple of blocks away. It was past 7 pm. It was the month of March and early spring, a time when it is supposed to be pleasant and cool, but is seldom so in reality. Located by the coast in southern India, the vast township of Sriharikota is generally hot and sultry throughout the year, often registering above normal temperatures. The ISRO Complex, also known as the Satish Dhawan Space Centre, was a fortress of sorts, being the hub of the nation's prestigious rocket launch activity. The sprawling estate wedged in-between the Bay of Bengal on its eastern side and the spectacular Pulicat Lake on the west was a high security zone protected by an army of commandos armed to their teeth.

Successive ISRO chairpersons had worked tirelessly to transform the campus into a rainforest with a variety of flora and fauna. For the fortunate residents of ISRO, it was nothing short of 'heaven' on earth. That evening in question though, the scientist did not come across anyone on the deserted road. From a distance, he could hear faint mellifluous tones of a *shehnai* coming from one of the houses in the employees' colony. The particular musical instrument, he knew, was usually played on auspicious occasions. He silently nodded in appreciation of the instrumentalist's expertise in navigating through an octave of complex notes of the Poorvi raga.

Dr Rangarajan reached his official residence. His wife Sangeetha was away in Bangalore spending time with their son, who worked for Infosys. For the past week, the scientist had been staying alone. He unlocked the front door and switched on the lights. Dropping the keys in a tray next to the main entrance, he sat on the sofa and closed his eyes. The silence calmed his mind. A couple of minutes later, the serenity of the night was disturbed by the jarring sound of something hitting the floor with a thud in his bedroom. He guessed it to be a book or a vase that had landed softly on the carpet.

Intrigued, he went to investigate the source of the noise. No sooner had he entered the room, when someone pounced on him from behind and pushed him on to the bed. He was instantly blindfolded with a plastic carry bag and punched hard on his back. Anticipating a shriek, the assailant had put his hand on Dr Rangarajan's mouth. The scientist's cry of anguish came out as a muffled squeak.

Agonising seconds passed that seemed like an eternity. When he was almost certain of death by strangulation, the assailant released his grip and spun him around on the bed sharply. He removed the blindfold and their eyes met for the first time, face-to-face in close range. Dr Rangarajan, recovered from the initial jolt, coughed and studied him. His attacker was tall, well-built, muscular and clad in black trousers with a matching full sleeved tee-shirt with a hood. Only his eyes and the tip of his nose were visible as he towered over the scientist.

'Who are you?' the scientist spluttered.

As if irritated by the question, the assailant whipped out a gleaming revolver in the dim light and pointed it between the scientist's eyes.

'No…no…please…please…let me go…,' Dr Rangarajan cried in desperation.

'No?' The assailant stopped dead in his tracks. Stunned by the bizzare reaction, Dr Rangarajan lay still, paralysed with fear.

The assailant politely enquired again gesturing in sign language, 'You mean you don't want to die?'

The scientist nodded, tears rolling down his cheeks, repeating, 'Please don't kill me.'

The assailant stepped back from the bed, and threw his hands up in mock despair. He paused dramatically, as if caught in a quagmire. He weighed the plea's pros and cons with mock gestures. A few seconds later, he said with a tone of finality:

'Fine, relax...take a deep breath...!'

He appeared apologetic for initiating the violent act without the victim's consent.

And before Dr Rangarajan could recover his wits and help himself off the bed, the assailant vanished, melting into the darkness as quietly as he had appeared.

A MINI emergency meeting was called in Dr Rangarajan's home. The chairman, Dr Anil Bhansal rushed to the aid of his seniormost colleague on hearing about the assault. The Chief Security Officer was summoned, who arrived with a group of commandoes as if they were entering a battle field.

Dr Rangarajan was attended to by the principal doctor on the campus who certified he was okay. 'He is just a bit dazed, sir. I will give him a mild sedative, and he'll be better by the morning,' he informed the chairman.

'Thank god!' Dr Bhansal exclaimed in relief. 'Ranga, don't worry my friend, I'm not moving from here until I get to the bottom of this,' he declared. The rest of ISRO's officials gathered in the hall stiffened in response. They knew the chairman to be a reticent man and they had never seen him so charged up.

The medical team moved out of the bedroom, allowing the scientist to rest. An armed security officer was placed right outside the bedroom.

'Will someone explain to me what's going on here?' the chairman asked the Chief Security Officer (CSO). 'Last, I checked, this was a supposed fortress. Didn't realise it is only as safe as a railway platform!'

'Sir,' the CSO stung by the sarcasm, began somberly, 'I can assure you no one can enter this site without proper scrutiny. This is ....'

'Cut the bullshit and come to the point?' the chairman visibly upset, interrupted him.

'I'll find out and revert soon, sir' he said.

'How much time do you need?' the chairman roared. 'Soon, near future? This isn't acceptable, officer.'

'I...I need...' the CSO muttered.

'You have one hour. I'll be waiting right here until you bring the culprit to me. Or else, heads will roll today. I'm reporting this matter to the PMO. I want this place protected by competent officers,' he shouted an ultimatum.

The CSO blinked helplessly. 'Sir, it may not happen within an hour, I am afraid, but I'll arrest the person very soon... sorry, at the earliest. Please give....'

The chairman's secretary came to the CSO's rescue. 'Sir, we will oversee the investigation. Meantime, you can rest at home, sir.'

'You guys have already wasted two minutes...,' the chairman said regretfully looking at his watch.

Sweating profusely, the CSO rushed outside with a few of his men following him.

Half an hour later, an official came up to the chairman, 'Sir we've a problem here...,' he said grimly.

'What?'

'Sir, one of our administrative staff's daughter got engaged this evening in the campus. The groom's relatives are stuck here since morning....'

The chairman gave him a cold look.

'Of course, with prior permission, sir....'

'Why are you telling me all this?'

'Sir, their function is over. The groom and his relatives want to leave... but are being held back, forcefully. Our employee's family are worried that in the light of this incident...,' he paused seeing the adverse effect his words were having on the boss. 'Sir, this might strain the delicate balance,' he quickly concluded.

'They can get the hell out,' the chairman thundered.

'Thank you, sir, very kind of you,' the official said and fled before the chairman could change his mind.

None had noticed that the camera team's assistant, employed for the engagement ceremony had been missing during the event. He had joined the unit only that morning. He returned quietly, just in time before their unceremonious departure. What's more, he carelessly dropped a bag, containing a black tee-shirt and a hood in the bin.

THE FOLLOWING morning, Dr Rangarajan woke up with a light headache. The events of the previous night had distressed him both physically and psychologically. A few points he could decipher with his sharp, scientifically inclined mind. Clearly, the unknown assailant had not come with an intention to kill him. He could've, if he had wanted to, but didn't. His sinister agenda was perhaps only to scare and soften him up. To a large extent, he conceded, the plan did succeed. The flawless execution of the assailant required meticulous planning to start with. He and his back up team, if at all he had any, had gone to great lengths to make it work and seem a simple, harmless intrusion.

But what was the assailant's motive? He was just one of the many scientists working for the Government of India. A nationalist at heart, he wouldn't hurt a fly, let alone an individual or an organisation. However, since the start of the year, he had this uneasy feeling that he was being watched. His hunch was rarely wrong. He had also mentioned this to the chairman, who had casually brushed it aside. He had never mentioned this to his family members, lest they panic. His phone too may have been tapped, but he wasn't sure.

In the aftermath of the mysterious assault, armed guards were posted around his home. It was too little, too late, the scientist thought. The horse had already bolted. The presence of guards was hardly reassuring and in fact made him more uneasy. He wanted to put the unpleasant experience behind and move on. Suddenly, he heard a commotion from the ground floor and heard the loud clicking of boots as his guards sprang to attention. The chairman, Dr Anil Bhansal was back in his home.

'Good morning, Ranga, hope you're feeling better, today,' Dr Bhansal greeted him with a smile and a warm handshake.

'Morning chairman, I'm fine,' he replied.

'That's my man, exactly what I wanted to hear,' the chairman responded.

'Now let's sort out a few things quickly. First, you can take it easy for a few days. And it's not a request, it's an order from the PMO. I briefed them last night. Secondly, they wanted to know if you still wanted to lead the delegation to Frankfurt for the European Space Agency meeting? I said, I would revert after checking with you.'

'You bet, I'm going to Frankfurt,' Dr Rangarajan stated categorically. 'I'm afraid I've to disobey the rest of your orders, Anil,' he replied, quietly. 'I'll be fine for only as long as I work. There's so much to do. Sitting idle at home will make me anxious. The ESA meeting is important for us. Any collaboration deal will benefit us enormously and push our space programme forward by leaps and bounds. And pardon the lack of humility, but I'm the best man to negotiate and get the job done for ISRO.'

'Ranga, you're tougher than I imagined! Great!' The chairman leaned forward and stroked his shoulder. 'I'm so proud of you. Moving forward, some bad news first. The security team have turned blank about your assailant, that too after my threats of suspending them all. Seems like an incompetent bunch of idiots,' he said, loud enough for the guards outside to hear his opinion. 'If you want, we can lodge a formal complaint with the local police. They could come in and investigate.'

'Not necessary,' Dr Rangarajan quickly replied. 'Nothing happened fortunately, so there's nothing to complain about.'

'Right, let me talk to Delhi on this. One theory Ranga...,' the chairman abruptly got up and closed the bedroom door, 'is that this is all about *Mission Antariksh*. As the date is drawing near, some enemies of the nation are apparently getting desperate. It's not a secret anymore that apart from the PM, and a few close aides, me and you...' he spoke in whispers. 'No one else is privy to this classified information. Add to this, the fluid scenario, general elections in two months' time, the whole atmosphere is bloody vitiated,' the chairman lamented.

Dr Rangarajan remained silent. He too had considered that angle. Suddenly, it occurred to him that he was the weakest link in that chain! He squirmed uncomfortably.

'But what the anti-national forces don't know,' the chairman's continued in a voice hard as steel, '... is that we aren't the type to buckle under such cheap threats. For us, the nation comes first over everything else including family.' He paused, then continued.

'Ranga, the launch is just three weeks from today. That's it, after that they can do whatever they want. We need to stay calm. We are on the cusp of making history!' he concluded animatedly.

'True...,' Dr Rangarajan mumbled, thinking about his wife and son in Bangalore.

He wasn't to know that much more agony and anxiety awaited the family later that afternoon.

IT WAS around 4 pm when Dr Rangarajan received a call from his son, Satish, whom he had fondly named after the great visionary of Indian space research, Satish Dhawan.

'*Appa*,' Satish's voice sounded tense, 'how are you?'

'I'm fine, how's *Amma* doing?' he enquired about his wife.

'She's good. All well here, but...I've to tell you about something...a strange incident that happened today,' Satish hesitated.

Dr Rangarajan felt his chest tighten. 'What?' he could barely be audible. His mouth had unexpectedly become dry and seemed incapable of producing sound waves.

'Don't panic, everyone is good...,' Satish's voice was reassuring, but it didn't comfort him much.

'Tell me what happened,' he snarled at his son.

'*Amma*, wanted to go out today. She was getting bored sitting at home. So, I dropped her off at Forum Mall on my way to office. Told her that I'd pick her up again in the afternoon. About half an hour later, I received a message from her phone.'

'Kidnapped your mom. She's going to die!'

'I thought it was a prank initially. But why would mom do that? I tried calling her. Her phone was switched off. I rushed back to the mall. And thereafter, along with my friends launched a search.

'Where is she now?' a distraught Ranga demanded.

'She's here, I'll give the phone to her,' Satish said.

'Hello! No need to worry, I'm fine,' Sangeetha spoke with a light chuckle! She found the incident amusing. 'Satish freaked out unnecessarily. I was fine. Bumped into an elderly lady who lives close by. She was also in the mall for window shopping. We went to a coffee shop and were chatting. Afterwards, she invited me to her home. I told her I'll inform my son first, but realised my phone was missing. We looked for it but could not find it. She was a very kind lady and offered her phone to call, but I didn't know the number. In any case, I knew he was going to come back to fetch me. She left me at the spot where Satish would pick me up. And you know what? It was she who found my phone. It had been in my bag all this time!' she laughed at her own forgetfulness.

Dr Rangarajan fumed, 'How many times should I tell you not to speak with strangers?' he commanded.

'Why are you angry? What is the matter?' Sangeetha asked, her tone suddenly serious.

'Nothing,' Dr Rangarajan murmured. 'Give the phone back to Satish.'

'Can you locate the woman who was with *Amma*?' he asked tersely.

'No… I mean we didn't look for her…*Amma* is fine right, why should we…?'

'Now, listen carefully,' he snapped, 'until the end of the month, *Amma* is not to go out anywhere alone. Am I clear?'

'*Appa*, you're freaking me out! And what is happening at the end of the month?'

'Don't ask stupid questions, just listen. Employ someone reliable to be with her, while you're at the office.'

'*Appa*… *Appa*…' Dr Rangarajan had disconnected. His

heart raced, just like an ignited rocket. Another 'threat' staged with incredible precision but ostensibly made to seem innocuous! A subtle message, implying that 'we can do anything.... to anyone in your family....'

As if on cue, exactly at that moment, the chairman, Dr Bhansal walked into Dr Rangarajan's office unannounced. It was rather unusual. Whenever the chairman needed something, it was he who would summon people to his office.

'Ranga, how's Sangeetha and Satish?' he asked casually.

'Huh' Dr Rangarajan glared at him with disbelief.

'Is everything...all right?' Dr Bhansal halted looking at his face.

'How did you know what happened...?'

'What happened to whom? When? Where?'

'Sangeetha and...and...Satish...?'

'You told me they were in Bangalore!'

'No, I did not.'

'You didn't?' the chairman seemed puzzled. 'Anyway, maybe someone did last night, but that's beside the point. How are they?'

'They're fine,' Dr Rangarajan muttered suspiciously.

'Right...,' the chairman continued, 'I just dropped by to tell you to ask Satish to take her to Forum Mall! My wife, Usha was there last month. Apparently it's a good place for passing time. Sangeetha could get acquainted with other ladies who share common interests.'

'That's it, thanks!' Dr Rangarajan brusquely got up and stormed to the door leaving the chairman gaping after him.

'Where are you going?' he asked, feeling insulted. It was a classic case of insubordination.

'Temple, sir, I need to pray for myself, my family and my country,' Dr Rangarajan replied without looking back.

There were only the empty walls to take in the chairman's puzzled look.

2

On the same night of the deadly assault on Dr Rangarajan, elsewhere in ISRO's residential quarters for employees, a poignant scene was being played out in one Radhakrishna's house. He was an administrative clerk in the management department.

Destiny had left 23-year-old Sithara with very little choice. Just as she wondered what more could go wrong in her life, her father lumbered into the room. Their modest but beautiful home amidst thick woods was part of the employees' colony. Perched on the window sill, she sobbed staring into the darkness aimlessly. She was adrift in her own world and didn't hear him come in. He had to clear his throat to announce his presence. Sithara got off the window and stood facing him like a hunted deer. She knew her moment of truth had arrived.

Mild-mannered simpleton, orthodox Brahmin by birth and practice, Radhakrishna had led a stress-free, modest life bereft of tall ambitions. Perhaps for the first time, he was confronted by a disproportionate crisis.

'Look sweetie,' he began sounding apologetic, 'you have to forgive me….' He had to pause, battling his emotions. 'I hope you have a wonderful life which I couldn't provide….,' he mumbled, unable to finish his sentence.

'*Nanna*, please don't cry…,' Sithara said, while running to hug her father.

He stopped her midway with a raised hand. 'Please… Don't make a scene here. I won't be able to handle,' he was apologetic for his inability.

Sithara closed her mouth in despair. She was being denied the basic birth right of a daughter.

'The point is, someday I must get your younger sister married, too. I know you wish good for her. But, your life's dark shadow shouldn't ruin hers. People here have long memories. God forbid,' he said, trailing off into silence.

'*Nanna*, your wish is my command,' Sithara said firmly. She wiped tears off her face and waited for his verdict.

'Find a job somewhere and be happy,' Radhakrishna delivered the ultimatum. She understood what it meant. 'Out of sight is out of mind they say,' he added.

'Sure *Nanna*, I'll go away and don't worry, I'll be fine…,' Sithara assured him.

He nodded faintly, but soon something bigger and heavier weighed him down. He made a hasty exit. Sujatha, Sithara's mother witnessing the father-daughter exchange from behind the door, hurried after him.

Sithara was alone again. Ironically, the expulsion notice served on her filled her with a strange sense of liberation. It helped clear the air. She was already contemplating her next move. She would miss the heavenly ISRO colony life. But then it wasn't the time for self-pity. Her madness had come back to haunt her. The universal folly of love! Unlike others of her age, she was paying a big penalty for it. Interrupting her stream of thoughts, her mother ambled in.

'Sweetie' she called out softly. 'I came to give you something...,' she announced. 'It isn't much, but...,' She held a bundle of coins along with a few crumpled currency notes tied in a transparent cloth like a ball.

'Thanks, *Amma,'* Sithara said accepting the treasure with eyes brimming with tears.

Sujatha paused at the door. 'Please don't tell Latha. You know her she'll be upset.'

'I won't, *Amma*.'

Sithara totaled the gift after her mom left. It was Rupees 508! More than sufficient for a one-way train fare to Chennai, her possible first stop, besides frugal meals for two or three days. She'd have to take life, one day at a time. She had faith in God. He would surely show the way, she comforted herself.

Ramesh, her ex-husband, the architect of her methodical destruction, had cleaned her up thoroughly. Even her father's savings had not been spared. She learnt later that he had abused her trust to fund his own illegal migration to Germany. Poor Radhakrishna had given in to his wannabe son-in-law's demands right until the day he had hurriedly arranged a sham wedding at the Registrar's office. Ramesh left for Germany the following day. A week later, the father-daughter duo travelled to Hyderabad to apply for Sithara's passport. When they arrived at the Passport Office, Ramesh gave instructions over the phone to pay a tout Rupees one lakh asserting that it was for Sithara's ticket to Germany. They paid up. Three weeks later when they returned to Hyderabad for passport collection, they discovered that they were the latest victims of a classic con job. Ramesh exonerated himself claiming that he too had become a victim of the tout's fraud. A fresh plea for Rupees two lakh to arrange Sithara's visa was made. 'It'll be done this time,' he assured. That's when Sithara became suspicious and spoke on her father's behalf.

'No,' she stated categorically.

'Then you may have to forget that a great life awaits you in Germany, Sithara,' Ramesh had threatened.

'To hell with Germany!' she had retorted. 'My family is more important than life with you.' Flustered by her sudden defiance, Ramesh quickly changed tack.

'Please understand, Darling,' he pleaded, 'I'm doing this for you. Otherwise, I'll be forced to marry a local here. That's the last option for me to become a legal citizen.'

'Do whatever you want, be happy and don't ever call me again,' Sithara had said firmly and disconnected the phone.

Later, when she went to Ramesh's house to collect her belongings, the diabolical plot became clearer. She overheard her mother-in-law brag about an Indian girl, Monica in Germany with whom Ramesh was apparently head over heels in love. His dalliance with Sithara was only a way to facilitate the Ramesh-Monica union.

'You've blown up the last chance to be my son's wife,' Ramesh's mom declared gesturing with her hands. 'My son is the star, not you,' she mocked. Sithara was used to hearing people mock her name which meant 'star' in Sanskrit. Her name had constantly been the butt of jokes, some good-humoured, others, plain nasty.

'Girls will queue up for him. You can never hope to find relevance in your life. Ah, in case you want a job here as a maid, I can make that happen,' she had said, supporting her son's treachery.

'Fallen stars' wither away at daybreak, ma'am. Your son will soon be extinct. Don't worry about me,' Sithara had said, giving it back to the nasty woman. Enraged, Ramesh's mom had dragged her out by her hair and thrown her out of the house. That was the end of the story.

Sithara grimaced at the bitter memory and absentmindedly fiddled with her long tresses. She recalled Ramesh mentioning that her long hair was the primary reason that he had fallen for her. Sithara now suddenly stood up and fetched scissors before proceeding to cut her hair up to her shoulders. Her sister, Latha, who had just come into the room shrieked in shock, 'What are you doing?'

'Getting ready for a new life!'

'You're mad, please don't do that' Latha pleaded, but it was too late.

'HEY, ARE you aware of the latest news doing the rounds in the colony? Something terrible happened in one scientist's home. Apparently, they tried to kill him…,' Latha divulged later that night.

'What?' Sitara exclaimed, suddenly attentive. 'Who? Which scientist?'

'The *Saar* who gave you the first prize in the singing competition last year.'

'Dr Rangarajan uncle?'

'Yeah, yeah. Same people were saying he's badly hurt.'

'Oh no he's a good man,' she cried. 'Have they taken him to hospital?'

'Don't know, but there's lot of commotion around his bungalow. Lots of cars, security…'

'My god!' Sithara exclaimed, 'I know him well. He comes to Laxmi Narayan temple regularly. He quietly listens to my songs. Come, let's go and see for ourselves.'

'Not a good idea. Mom won't allow that,' Latha said to her.

'We'll tell her something…at least we will know what's happening inside, come *na*…,' Sithara pulled her younger sister. They ran towards the scientist's home like excited children.

DR RANGARAJAN got off the car in a huff, near the pathway leading to the temple. As usual, he wanted to walk from his office, but his security team would've none of it. Officers assigned for his protection tried to follow him inside.

'I want to be alone, here. In peace… Do you mind?'

The officers hesitated.

'None can harm me in HIS presence, so please…' he told them firmly. They glanced at each other and reluctantly held themselves back.

Sithara spotted the scientist from afar. She was pleasantly surprised to find that he looked hail and healthy. The previous night, she and her sister weren't allowed to go anywhere close to his home.

Inside the temple, she waited in a corner until he had finished his prayers in solitude and squatted on the marble floor, leaning his back against a pillar. She approached him with trepidation.

'Good evening, sir, I hope you're okay now?' she said respectfully when he looked up.

'Sir, I heard about the horrific incident and was very worried for you.'

'You are… the singer, right?'

'Yes sir, Sithara is my name,' she reintroduced herself, glad that he was able to recognise her.

'What's with this new hairdo…?' he asked hesitatingly. 'I couldn't place you.'

She giggled.

'Come… come, sit,' he said making place for her to sit down next to him. 'I'm fine, thanks.'

She fidgeted with her hair, 'Just for a change, sir.'

'Umm…It's nice,' he reaffirmed.

'Thank you, sir,' she acknowledged the compliment like

any young woman. 'Sir, I cannot imagine how frightening it must've been for you. How can anyone think of harming you? I mean… a good human being like you….'

The scientist shrugged his shoulders. For the first time in thirty-six hours, he felt he was having a conversation with a genuine human being who really cared.

'Well…,' he paused for a moment searching for an appropriate response. 'Humans are exposed to motives all the time in our wakeful state… And yet only a few of us succumb to them and commit crimes….'

'But what could be the motive to assault you, sir?'

'Greed, power, money, plenty of reasons. They can make people do funny things, don't you think?' he retorted, with a wry smile. He couldn't recall the last time he had actually smiled.

'I don't know…sir' Sithara shrugged in disagreement. 'But, I'm relieved you're good now,' she beamed. 'God is great. He will look after you and your family. I will definitely pray for your well-being, sir,' she continued.

He felt a radiant sun shine on him. 'Thanks, that's so sweet of you.'

'Ok sir, I shall take your leave,' she said and stood up.

'Hey!' he signaled her to continue sitting, 'Are you in such a tearing hurry?'

'Not at all, sir, I thought you're busy.'

'No, I'm not,' he said and felt good when she sat down. 'I remember you addressing me as 'uncle'. When did that become, sir?'

'No, sir… sorry…uncle, you are a big man, so…,' she said.

'Nobody is big or small, dear,' he said humbly. 'Only deeds matter.'

'True, uncle.'

A long pause ensued between them. Time seemed to stand still. He didn't mind. Nor did she.

'Do you still sing?'

'I do, uncle, but only occasionally. So many problems in life, no time actually,' she said with a certain sense of dignity and acceptance.

'Ah! ridiculous excuse!' he said, expressing his disapproval. 'You found time to experiment with your hair, didn't you? Look, you're a gifted singer. I was particularly impressed with the rendition in *Sivaranjini Raagam* in the competition's final round. It's my favourite *raagam,* you know,' Dr Rangarajan said as his mind drifted into the tranquil world of music.

'Thank you, uncle. You're so simple, kind… generous,' Sithara instinctively bent down and touched his feet in reverence.

'Hey! God bless you,' Dr Rangarajan said, feeling awkward. Again silence.

'Can I ask you something, uncle?'

'Sure you can,' he responded immediately, 'what is it?'

'Can you recommend me for a job? I badly need one,' she said sounding anxious. 'Not here in ISRO though… Somewhere far away like in Chennai or elsewhere, any job.'

He studied her intently. 'Any particular reason you don't want to be here?' he asked.

'It's a long story, uncle.'

'Tell me about it. I've the time to listen, if you don't mind.'

'I was in love with a boy. He abandoned me three days after our marriage for another girl. Basically, he cheated me and my dad…of lots of money…,' her words trailed off. She was silent.

'Ohh…sorry!' Dr Rangarajan said.

'It's okay, uncle. He's now in Germany. And my father wants me to leave the house because my being here can ruin my sister's chances of getting a good boy for marriage. Can't blame daddy. He's right only, no? What can he do if my fate is like that?' she narrated her story laced with pure innocence and profound honesty. She didn't try to hide her flaws and readily took the entire blame on herself.

'I'm so sorry,' he exclaimed. 'I'm going to Germany in two days' time. Do you want me to talk to this…boy… your husband?'

'No, no, uncle… I don't want to ever see him again,' she dismissed the idea vehemently. 'It's okay, uncle. If you can't find me a job, I'll do something on my own. Sorry for bothering you,' she was repentant and yet graceful. No pretense but genuine emotions.

'I can lend you some money,' he offered. 'You can return later.'

'Thanks uncle, but no need.

He thought for a moment.

'Alright then, I'll give you a job, Sithara,' he said instinctively. 'Will you work for me?'

Her face lit up, 'Yes! But what should I do?'

'Good question,' Dr Rangarajan said. He took out Rupees 10,000 from his pocket and put in in her hand. 'Not for me actually, but from now on, you are employed for the country!'

'Really?' she cried with her gaze stuck on the cash in her hand. 'So much money?'

'Um…it's for you to buy a smart phone. Meet me here at the same time tomorrow. I'll give you a sim card. It's going to be a secret assignment. Actually, a backup. Any time after tomorrow and until the end of the month, I might pass on instructions or documents by email, SMS or simply message on WhatsApp. You need to keep it in safe custody and follow my instructions in total secrecy.'

'I'm… flattered, uncle, thank you…but…but not sure, if I can do that,' she hesitated with self-doubt and disbelief.

'Why not?' Dr Rangarajan questioned her. 'You know, in rocket science, when faced with a challenge, we ask ourselves, "Is this possible?" If it is, we go ahead no matter what. So, ask yourself, is it possible?'

'Uncle, I'm not saying it's impossible,' she retorted swiftly.

'There you go!' Dr Rangarajan grinned. 'You are a quick learner.' She smiled back, realising the importance of this simple change in perspective.

'But I've a question.'

'Yes?'

'What will be my working hours and salary, uncle?'

He laughed. 'Don't worry about all those things now. You'll get what's sufficient to lead a decent, respectable life. Happy?'

'Yes, happy,' her smile warmed his heart. She gave him a thumbs up sign.

'By the way, no one should know about our arrangement,' he cautioned her. 'It's for your own safety you know... I need someone here whom I can trust.'

'Sure uncle.'

'And… no worries, this rule is not for ever. Only until 27 March.'

'Oh! What happens on 27 March, uncle?'

'It's better if you don't know….'

Sithara's eyes welled up, 'Sure, uncle, don't tell me. Thank you so much for your trust and faith in me.'

'Come on, I know you.'

'I'll not disappoint you, uncle.'

'I know that too, Sithara,' he said and stood up. He walked away without looking back.

SITHARA SET out early from home the next day. She travelled to the nearby town of Nellore and bought a mobile phone for ₹7,500, returned home and waited for the evening. She arrived at the temple, an hour earlier.

The temple priest, a longtime acquaintance, enquired casually, 'Sithara, here in the evening? What's the matter?'

'Nothing, just thought of some music practice in His presence,' she replied casually.

'Good, good. You can also give me a helping hand while you're practising,' he said chirpily.

'Okay, sir, anything for the Lord,' she said plunging into floral decoration arrangements. She hummed a devotional song while she worked.

'Good evening, Sithara,' a familiar voice greeted her. She turned around.

'Good evening, uncle,' she said spiritedly and rummaged through her purse for the new mobile phone. She was about to excitedly reveal its features when he gestured her to put it away. She hurriedly hid the package. Right behind them was the temple priest waiting for Dr Rangarajan.

After offering prayers, Sithara and Dr Rangarajan settled down in a corner of the temple premises.

'Glad you got it done,' he said checking the instrument. He handed her phone back along with a sim card. 'Remember, this number is only for one-way communication. You cannot use this phone for your personal needs.'

'Oh,' she looked disappointed.

'Second, any person calling this number, will most likely know you. So, don't ever mention your identity. If he or she asks for your id, it means trouble and danger. Don't talk, disconnect immediately. Is that clear?'

'Yes, uncle,' Sithara said, listening intently.

'There's also a chance that no one may ever call! You see, this is all a contingency plan, until I return from Germany.'

'Okay uncle.'

'Put the sim in the phone right away. Let me text you. We'll make sure it's working.'

'Okay, uncle,' she said and did as instructed.

'One more important point. Don't ever delete a message or data or whatever lands on your phone…every bit of information is important.'

'Okay, uncle.'

'I've something else for you,' he said and handed over a packet with cash. 'You'll need this for any task I may assign. This is for your personal needs also, consider it as an advance against your pay.'

'Oh my god!' Sithara exclaimed looking at the wad of cash. 'This is more than even the chairman of ISRO earns, uncle!'

He laughed at her naivety.

'Not really, dear,' he said. 'Right now, you're on probation. Remember you're working for the Government of India. We come under the Department of Space and report directly to the Prime Minister of India. We are answerable only to the PMO, no less.'

'Understood, uncle,' she said suddenly feeling important.

'Good'

'Uncle, will I get an appointment letter?'

'All that after I return, don't think too far ahead. We'll cross one bridge at a time. You may get a different assignment when the time comes,' he said. 'Anything else?'

'Just one more thing uncle, if you don't mind. Wanted to know…. This is actually away from the topic….'

'What is it?'

'Did they catch the man who attacked you?'

'No,' Dr Rangarajan said, his face turning grim.

'Oh! They don't know who he is or where he came from?'

'Actually, they know how he came in here....'

'How?'

'There was some function in the colony that evening. He apparently sneaked in as one of the guests or some part of the engagement team. Something like that....'

'Oh,' she exclaimed, her face turning pale. 'But who is he?'

'No one has an answer for that, yet,' he said seemingly withdrawn.

'What did he look like, uncle?' she persisted with curiosity borne out of pure innocence.

'Hmmm,' he thought back, 'it's strange no one asked me this question. He was wearing a tight fitting black full sleeved tee-shirt and trousers. Tall, about 6 feet, I would imagine. Muscular, trim body, covered from head to toe. But in those ninety seconds, I also noticed that he possibly had a congenital malformation at birth.'

'What's that... uncle?'

'His left leg was a bit shorter than his right. So, when he stood upright, he tended to lean towards his left making the deformity seem normal. He was also perhaps left-handed because he shifted the revolver from his right to the left hand very quickly.'

Sithara felt a shiver up her spine on hearing the graphic description. She wished she hadn't brought up the subject. He noticed her discomfort and quickly changed the subject.

'Anyway...you shouldn't be wasting your time on such irrelevant things,' he reprimanded her gently.

'Sorry for asking, uncle.'

'Never mind,' he reassured her.

'I'll be leaving for Chennai soon, uncle,' she said.

'Join some music classes there. There are plenty of teachers. You need to nurture the talent God has gifted you,' he urged.

'With your blessings, I will, uncle.'

'You can find shelter in one of the women's hostels there. Put the money I gave you to good use,' he advised.

'Thank you so much, uncle,' she said gratefully moved by his generosity. 'When are you leaving for Germany?'

'Saturday.'

'I can come and meet you after you return, right?'

'Of course, you can. I'll message you. Okay dear, I must leave now,' he said exiting the temple precincts hurriedly.

She watched him from a distance as he got into his car followed by his security men and drive away. Her phone beeped seconds later. It was a message from him, '*God bless you.*'

She felt truly blessed with a sense of overwhelming gratitude. It was as if she was at the crossover point and ready for a fresh start. And he had come like a messenger of God. Start of a new chapter in her life.

In the car, Dr Rangarajan wondered if he had successfully camouflaged his noble intentions of keeping 'hope' alive in a sincere young girl caught in a personal turmoil. Youngsters like her needed to be encouraged and nurtured. The girl's self-respect would've compelled her to make excuses for accepting cash, even if given on humanitarian grounds. She could have refused such a bid and hence he had to think of an ingenious alternative. Indeed, in future if she did prove herself to be worthy, it wouldn't be difficult for him to find her an appropriate job. But that would be later, of course.

3

A week earlier… Somewhere near Delhi

So many unsavoury events in the country in February 2019 had set in motion a profound turmoil in public perception and parties trying to stay relevant in the ever-churning political cauldron. A terrorist attack sponsored and coordinated allegedly by Pakistan had resulted in the death of forty Indian security personnel. India exercised its right to retaliate and wreaked revenge with air strikes in Balakot, deep inside enemy territory. Ironically, the action had resulted in boosting the PM and his government's credibility, exponentially! He gained the respect and approval of citizens even while he was seeking a second term in office. If this wasn't enough to demoralise the opposition which was aiming to dethrone him, an Indian pilot captured by Pakistan had to be released under sustained international pressure on 1 March. It was unprecedented ignominy for our neighbouring nation.

A few days later, the opposition political parties had huddled together at a secret venue on the outskirts of Delhi for a strategic discussion. Their agenda was to formulate a counter strategy, if any, and find ways to deal with the rapidly deteriorating situation in the country from their perspective.

One prominent leader from Delhi was blunt and categorical in his opening statement, 'If we don't team up and work together then we might as well look for some alternate profession. This is the last chance, gentlemen, so let's put up a united front to defeat the PM.'

A leader from Uttar Pradesh, while appreciating the core agenda, had wanted to know how it could be achieved. 'It's all fine talk, but what are the issues to oppose? Without a rallying point, we are like headless chickens in these times.'

Another of their ilk from southern India concurred but was more concerned about an immediate issue at hand, 'From where's the chicken curry coming for tonight's dinner? Only after good food can I actually think,' he had said, sardonically. Everyone glared at him.

'What?' he scowled back at them. 'We're all made differently, okay.'

The Bengal politician, a sagacious woman, brokered peace between them, 'Please, I request you all to be serious. This meeting is not a joke. '*Baba ki hoche*...,' she exclaimed aloud, 'it's like a circus....'

A seasoned and erudite politician from Maharashtra chipped in diverting attention with his theory. He said, 'To me it seems as if Pakistan is fixing the match in the PM's favour! But why the hell would they do that?'

'They hate him more than us,' the Bengal lioness added.

'Exactly,' the Maharashtrian concurred. Meantime, others argued among themselves on the earlier gourmet remark. 'Gentlemen, if we fight among ourselves, we will never succeed,' an astute politician observed.

After a few more appeals from other sections, they settled down.

The Maharashtrian took centerstage, 'Indeed, our duty to the people of India is to counter the government's policies if and when they are anti-people. But, it must be said, whatever has happened since last month, the PM has reacted rightly and boldly and gave a fitting reply to our common enemy. Of course, luck has also favoured him,' he concluded, rather ruefully.

The Delhi man objected, 'Are you with us or him? Our neighbouring country seems to be more confused than us!'

'I don't know…,' the Maharashtrian gave up.

The emboldened Delhi man put his point across. 'Anyone in the PM's chair would've reacted the same way. What's the big fuss about?'

A politician from Bihar woke up from his slumber and asked, 'But *Sirji*, did you?

'What?'

'When you were in power, did you?'

The Delhi man's face turned red, 'Excuse me,' he said, lamely.

'You didn't have the balls,' the Bihar man stated bluntly.

The Maharashtra senior stepped in with a terse, 'Gentlemen and ladies, this is not the time or place for a *tu-tu-mein-mein* match.'

With deep mutual mistrust and more than one axe to grind among themselves, the politicians who had gathered began to wonder—what the hell were they doing there in the first place?

'With great difficulty, we could hold back the construction of the *Ram Mandir*, until after the elections,' the UP politician reminded the gathering. He had been quiet all along. 'If we allow him to get away with a second term, the temple will be done, and there will be no stopping him after that,' he wailed ominously.

'What's gone is gone. There's no point fighting over what could've been done. We all have assembled here to arrive at a minimum common agenda to work together. Just sixty days to go before people in this country start pressing the buttons on the EVM machines. This is no time for infighting,' a suave politician from central India reminded them.

A politician from South India, Senthil, cleared his throat wanting to say something.

'There he goes again. There's a problem with the chicken curry, I suppose,' an anonymous voice bemoaned.

'I've some bad news to share,' Senthil began on a gloomy note that got everyone's attention.

'You're the bad news! What good can be expected from you?' someone echoed.

That didn't discourage the man from Chennai to make

his point. 'There are confirmed reports that we'll soon hear a Diwali firecracker, from the south, by the end of the month!'

'What the hell does he mean?' the startled Delhi man commanded.

'We are in March...Diwali is in November. Are you drunk?' the perplexed Bihar man asked.

'Friends, to be precise, something is cooking in ISRO, which could potentially catapult the PM to 300 seats in the Parliament, I've been reliably informed,' he declared. 'I'll give you a clue,' he turned to his sarcastic Bihar colleague and gestured how a particular firecracker would blast off. Diwali rocket! Boom! Senthil gestured and laughed savagely, savouring their incredulous looks.

Everyone's face fell. Shoulders drooped.

'But friends, relax,' the Chennai man cheered them, 'I've good news also. We've identified a weak link in the chain. A scientist by the name of Dr Rangarajan. We are working on him. He'll sing for us.'

'Heard ISRO scientists are very patriotic and have scant respects for politicians,' the Bihar man said pondering on what's left in India to be nationalistic about. 'If he chooses to ignore you, what then?'

'We'll deal with him suitably,' Senthil said firmly. 'If necessary, we can silence him.'

'Dr *Wrong Rajan*...!' the UP man scowled, 'would serve him right. Why can't he make rockets and mind his own business? Why interfere with our work?' he asked. Most ignored him.

'How can you be so cool about this?' the curious Bihar man wanted to know.

'Good question,' the Tamil leader explained, 'because no matter what, your PM or any of the north Indian parties can't win in my state without our tacit support. Dravidian politics is unique and untouchable on our turf. We might fight amongst ourselves but will not allow an outsider to come and rule over us. Of course, we might not be able to make an impact at the national level, but who cares?'

'You can more or less say the same for my state also,' the Bengali woman messiah added.

'But,' Senthil paused, and added, like an afterthought, 'if you people do have some plan, we will be glad to help, *Vannakkam,*' he uttered the respectful Tamil greeting used both for welcoming as well as leave-taking.

'If only we could find common ground and fight the enemy as one unit,' the Delhi leader urged, still hopeful of a consensus.

'Well said,' the Maharashtrian affirmed. 'That way, we can share the pie.'

'So, let me know when you do find this "common ground",' the Bengal lady said gesturing with inverted commas for added impact as she got up, abruptly. She had had enough.

'Thank you for coming, ma'am,' the Maharashtrian acknowledged her with a 'Namaste'. She didn't bother to look back.

The leaders from Bihar and Tamil Nadu left shortly afterwards.

'In the event, you're able to find something against this despicable PM, I'm extending an open invitation for a fifty-fifty seat-sharing alliance in my state,' the UP leader stated and left the venue. Only the Delhi and the Maharashtrian politicians now remained.

MANIKRAO KHARMATE, Maharashtra's supreme leader pondered over the ISRO information he had just heard, 'I don't believe space research scientists could come up with a magic potion for the PM.'

'Me too, but we can't be caught napping,' Rohit Sachdeva, the National contender from Delhi responded. 'It's better to be sorry now, than later. Besides, we know this PM will shamelessly take credit for the successes of the Army, scientists, sportspersons,' he scowled contemptuously.

'ISRO reports directly to him in total secrecy. On second thoughts, I'm now seriously concerned by the proposed spectacular endeavour that the idiot was talking about. What if it's a guided missile programmed to hit Pakistan?' Kharmate wondered aloud.

'Not likely,' Rohit Sachdeva said, dismissing the idea as preposterous. 'But we must find out. It shouldn't be difficult if we put the right men on the job to work on the scientist. It can also be arranged,' he added, offering a subtle hint.

'Leave it to me. It's a pleasure working with someone with your resources,' Kharmate expressed appreciatively. 'I've had the good fortune of interacting with your family for many decades now.'

'We're natural allies, Manikrao Saab,' Rohit beamed. 'You should lead the next government at the Centre.'

'Let's first defeat him,' Kharmate said, shaking hands warmly. 'I'll tackle the scientist first.'

'Don't kill him,' Rohit cautioned.

'No, no… I'll scare the daylights out of him, that's all.'

The two leaders stood up and hugged each other before parting.

'Will keep you posted on all developments on the Diwali of the south!' Kharmate said getting into his car. Rohit Sachdeva acknowledged, flashing a 'V' sign with his hands, before turning to look for his car.

'Where the hell is my driver?' Sachdeva said to his staff.

The staff ran searching for him. The driver came rushing in to take his place behind the wheel, '*Sorry Sirji, toilet ke liye gaya tha….*'

'*Chal Chutiye*,' the politician swore disgustedly.

None paid attention to the fact that the 'alleged driver' was a temporary employee who had joined work only that morning. More importantly, he was missing for a long time when the secret meeting was underway and emerged just at the end of it!

Present Time...

The countdown at Sriharikota had already begun, forty hours prior to the launch. Dr Rangarajan was on the final check of the parameters in the lead up to India's Geosynchronous Satellite Launch Vehicle (GSLV)-F 11 that would place the 2250-kg pay load GSAT -7A into a geosynchronous Transfer Orbit. GSLV–F 11 would lift off from ISRO's Second Launch Pad (SLP) at the Satish Dhawan Space Centre. The GSAT -7A's belly had been customised specifically for military operations. The satellite, once in orbit would interlink all the ground-based radars, airbases and aircraft of the Indian Air Force for surveillance. It would vastly maintain their air superiority over the enemy with real-time aircraft-to-aircraft communication. The targeted apogee of the satellite was anywhere between 33,000 to 40,000 km. The idea was to use less fuel to carry out orbit-raising manoeuvres, thereby enhancing the life of the spacecraft. As it is, the mission life of GSAT – 7A was expected to be eight years.

The satellite's working relied on sound converted into signal which the IAF jets transmit to the satellite. On its part, the satellite would amplify the signals transmitted by the jets and change their frequency. The signals would then reach the receiver antenna in another aircraft where they are converted back to sound. The same could also be picked up by antennas on the ground.

For Dr Rangarajan, it was a matter of honour and pride that under his watch, the GSAT – 7A would be the heaviest satellite being launched by GSLV with an indigenously developed cryogenic stage! The launch was scheduled for the next night. Many IAF officers were already in ISRO's campus to witness the launch.

Soon it was launch time. T-4, T-3, T-2, T-1…

'Launch!' T+1… T+2…

Dr Rangarajan's favourite part in the launch was the visual of the fire spewing out from the engine. A thunderous roar of yet another man-made machine soared into the skies. The first 200 seconds after the ignition were important. The sky around the launch pad suddenly turned orange as if it was evening again! An instant applause broke out in the visitor's gallery.

'Not yet, gentlemen,' Dr Rangarajan thought.

Seconds passed. The lady announced the successful GS1 separation and GS2 Ignition. A couple of minutes later, the GS2 separation happened. Dr Rangarajan began to relax. The announcement of CUS ignition came on. Two minutes later, the CUS burnt out and finally it was the GSAT -7A separation! Visuals of the separation were clearly visible on the giant screen in the Mission Control Room. Applause again. The mission, officially, was a success! The IAF officers shook hands with the ISRO scientists. The chairman, Dr Anil Bhansal got ready to address the gathering as news channels focused their cameras on him. His job done, Dr Rangarajan quietly slipped out of the Mission Control Room and headed home.

After the assault incident, a new protocol was in place. A

couple of officers would check and sanitise the entire house before he was allowed to step in. One security officer usually accompanied him right until his bedroom and left only after he was convinced that everything was fine. Dr Rangarajan found it irksome but unavoidable considering what had happened. Just when he thought, the occasion called for a celebration, his phone rang. Private number calling it said on the display.

'Congratulations, Dr Rangarajan,' the voice greeted.

'Who's this?' he asked curtly.

'Really, does it matter? Let's just say, I'm also a proud Indian, chatting with a great rocket scientist of our times.'

It didn't take long for Dr Rangarajan to realise he was talking to the perpetrator of the recent assault on himself and his family. He wished he had the wherewithal to prerecord the conversation. It was too late for that.

'Proud Indian? You're a disgrace to India,' he retorted, keeping his emotions in check.

The man chuckled, 'I think you've taken my mischief to heart. It's the amusing part of my job. It's tough otherwise to make a living in this competitive world. Everyone can't be a scientist like you earning in millions,' he said, in a mock-humble tone.

'That's true. Sadly, you must be unemployed and therefore, desperate for cash. You can take an instant loan from me. Don't be ashamed. I can lend you a thousand bucks. Will that do?'

The scientist could hear the laboured breathing on the other side. He had successfully managed to get under the skin of his assailant.

'And speaking of your "mischief", frankly, it's irksome. Now if you'll excuse me, it has been a wonderful day. There's a rare feeling of joy when you do your bit for the beloved nation. Of course, these things are beyond morons like you,' he said and scoffed loudly. He wanted the derision in his voice to be heard.

The caller abruptly disconnected.

Dr Rangarajan checked his phone. The call's duration was for 2 minutes 23 seconds. He had given a fitting response exhibiting bravado. He felt better. Now the cat was set among the pigeons. He had to be prepared for the retaliation. He was reasonably secure and had already warned his son. As a backroom exigency, there was Sithara too. More, however, needed to be done.

He picked up his phone and called Pratap Suri, his go-to man in the PMO.

'Congratulations, Dr *Saab*,' Suri greeted warmly as soon as he picked up, 'PM has been informed. He's so happy and proud of you.'

'Thanks, we are just doing the duty expected of us,' he said.

'What can I do for you, Dr *Saab*?'

'Umm, a few important things actually,' the scientist started. 'I'm sure you've come to know by now. There was an ugly incident here.'

'Yes, yes, I know about that,' Suri turned serious.

'I want my phone calls to be monitored. Need a report at the end of the day mentioning who called and from where.'

'Huh!' Suri held his breath, and added, 'Sure, no problem.'

'Secondly, I need personal surveillance equipment for self-use. In case I want to record a suspicious activity around me or take pictures. I'm leaving for Germany on Saturday and would appreciate it if it reaches me before that.'

'It'll be done,' Suri assured.

Another 36 hours to go before he boarded the flight to Germany.

THE NEXT morning, Dr Rangarajan introspected. He hadn't heard again from his son or wife in two days. No news meant good news. All good in Bangalore, he presumed. He contemplated taking the day off. He had a bit of packing left. Around 10 am, he got a call from Dr Bhansal, the chairman.

'Ranga, is it possible for you to drop by my office?' he asked.

'Yeah, sure,' he answered out of courtesy but groaned inwardly. 'I'll reach in twenty minutes.'

'Thanks, there's a distinguished gentleman from Chennai, whom I want you to meet.'

Who could it be, Dr Rangarajan thought. The chairman of ISRO had regular visits by VIPs from all over the world. He got dressed and drove up to the office. He found a sleek SUV parked in the foyer with an official government of Tamil

Nadu emblem along with an escort vehicle. Whomsoever his boss was to introduce was most certainly a politician in power. He was never fond of them. Walking into the chairman's chamber, his eyes fell on a 50-year-old, fair-complexioned, thick set man with a pot belly, sleekly dressed with polished shoes. He sat across the chairman's table. From his attire resembling a latter-day technocrat, Dr Rangarajan could confirm that the guest was indeed, a formidable politician.

'Ahh… come in,' the chairman beamed and got up. Dr Rangarajan occupied an empty chair at a handshaking distance from the visitor. He noticed the guest hadn't moved in his chair.

'Meet Mr Senthil, Rajya Sabha Member of Parliament from Chennai,' the chairman formally introduced his guest.

Dr Rangarajan nodded, 'Hello'. The MP nodded back. The mutual dislike was palpably obvious.

Breaking the ice, the chairman said, 'My blue-eyed scientist is also from your state, sir,' and laughed as if it were the joke of the year.

'*Vanakkam*, how are you?' the MP spoke in Tamil.

'There you go!' the chairman chuckled. 'Naturally you would both speak in your mother tongue,' he remarked.

'No sir,' Dr Rangarajan shot back. 'It is basic courtesy to converse in a language known to all. I prefer English.'

'These north Indians have no idea of our heritage,' the MP said to him in Tamil.

Dr Rangarajan translated it verbatim for the chairman.

The response was a cheeky laugh, 'No, we do. We certainly know if you're speaking against us,' Dr Anil Bhansal said. 'Anyway, I better get going. I have an important video conference waiting to happen. Don't want to come in between two Tamilians chatting in your own tongue.'

He turned to his colleague, and said, 'Mr Senthil has come all the way from Chennai to meet you.'

'Really, for what do I owe this honour?' Dr Rangarajan responded mockingly.

'That you'll have to ask him. Please show him around our Launch Pads. Apparently, Mr Senthil has been fascinated with rockets from a very young age.' The chairman got up from his seat and shook hands with the MP, and left the room.

Exiting the chairman's office, the two men's conversation shifted to Tamil.

'You people are doing great work here, Ranga,' the MP said referring to him by his first name.

'Thanks sir, but I prefer being called by my full name,' Dr Rangarajan said as they strolled out into the sprawling corridors. 'You did not come here to see launch pads, did you?'

'You're sharp,' Senthil acknowledged. 'North Indians are not nice people, you know. They think of themselves as superior to us,' the MP began on a sour note.

'That's strange coming from a parliamentarian representing the people of India. I don't think that's the case. I've great friends coming from all parts of India!' Dr Rangarajan gave it back, tit for tat. Senthil's face turned purple.

'I'm trying to talk to a Tamil brother here,' he roared.

'And I'm speaking as an Indian.'

'Open your eyes and see the reality, sir. Our ideology is to fight the people who impose things on us unilaterally,' he said. 'Your PM is autocratic and doesn't care about us.'

'Seriously, is he not your PM, too?' Dr Rangarajan was running short of patience. His mobile phone rang interrupting the chat. He ignored it.

The MP urged him to take the call. Surprised, Dr Rangarajan looked at the display. It was his son! He answered suspiciously.

'*Appa*?' Satish sounded anxious.

'All well, Satish?'

'Yes, yes no worries,' he replied, realising his dad's unease. 'Just wanted to check with you. Did you transfer ₹25 lakh to my account today?'

'No, I didn't!' Dr Rangarajan cried out involuntarily.

'I did,' the MP privy to their conversation said.

'I'll call you back in a while, Satish,' Dr Rangarajan said to his son and disconnected and glared at the MP. If his eyes could shoot, the MP would have been dead meat!

'What do you want?'

'He had applied for a loan to buy a flat, right? Consider this an interest-free loan. You can pay me back,' Senthil said casually.

'Who do you think you are?'

'Calm down, Ranga sir!'

'Don't call me Ranga!'

'Okay…okay, think of it as a gift from the people of Tamil Nadu.'

'For what?'

'For information of course! What do you people call it? Moon, Mars…Ahh…Mission…!' He froze midway because he saw Dr Rangarajan recording on his phone camera. 'What are you doing?' he shrieked in panic.

'Please continue…What do you want to know? You were saying some Mission…?' Dr Rangarajan urged him. The MP quickly recovered his poise.

'I was saying this ISRO campus is so beautiful and the nation is so proud of Tamils who excel here. Please stop recording Dr Rangarajan, you're embarrassing me,' he said in a bid to sound politically correct.

'Mr Senthil,' Dr Rangarajan put the phone away and confronted him. 'Unfortunately, you've picked the wrong guy. You'll not get anything out of me, nothing.'

'Your wish…I'm courteous to you. Tomorrow the North Indians will come in my place. They are nasty fellows. Rough and tough. I thought it was my duty to warn you as a Tamil.'

'So, you are the one who sent that goon to my house?' Dr Rangarajan asked.

'I don't know what you're talking about,' Senthil said, shrugging his shoulders.

'Right, Mr MP please get out of this campus before I call the security,' he thundered with gusto.

'Sad, very sad,' Senthil scowled. 'A super intelligent man like you doesn't understand the difference between a friend and an enemy. Anyway, if you change your mind, let me know,' he said and walked away.

Dr Rangarajan wished the recording equipment had been with him. He would've nailed the bastard. He called his son and asked him to reverse the credit at once and to send an email to the bank stating that the remittance was from an unknown, fictitious transferee.

He called Pratap Suri in the PMO and reported the MP Senthil's visit to him. He enquired about the status of the surveillance kit. Suri assured him that it would reach by the evening.

Incensed, he still felt hot under his collar. Damn, these bloody politicians!

4

Frankfurt International Airport

Jasmine Priya Samuel, born and raised in a Bangalore Protestant family, had attented Bishop Cotton Girl's School in the heart of the city. She was known as Jazz to most of her friends and family. Her father was the organist at St. Mark's Cathedral. Although Jazz was expected to excel in singing and playing the piano, she went on to win accolades in elocution, debates and sports. With a slim athletic figure and dusky skin to go with it, she was often mistaken for a famous Bollywood actor. In the early millennium, many German, English and American Pastors came visiting Bangalore. Jazz was held in awe by them and she felt at ease in their presence because of her metropolitan roots. It wasn't long before she aimed and cleared the qualifying exams to reach Germany as a student of merit on a scholarship in 2006. In München University, she got admission in her favourite subject, Earth Oriented Space Science and Technology.

It was in the University that Jasmine first chanced upon Tobias Rosenbuch, a handsome hunk, a German, who was immediately smitten by her sparkling eyes. Tobias was a research scholar in robotic engineering. The courtship that followed in the serene backdrop of the München campus was part of the university's romantic folklore. Theirs seemed like a match made in heaven. As soon as Tobias completed his studies, he proposed to Jasmine and they were soon married.

Tobias became the vice president in his father's company, Rosenbuch Industries dealing in automobile engineering parts and the couple moved to Frankfurt. Jasmine continued to pursue her interests in space technology while working part-time in the Indian Embassy. The couple were blessed with a baby girl, Niniya. The first and only setback in life for them was that Niniya, was discovered to be suffering from Autism Spectrum Disorder (ASD) and while no one could really explain why their little girl was suffering from ASD, deep within her, Jasmine would feel guilty—was it divine retribution for her wrong actions in the past?

Today, as the designated officer-in-charge for coordination with the Indian delegation of Space Research Scientists, Jasmine waited at the Arrival lounge of the Frankfurt airport for Dr Rangarajan's team to step out. An adorable child walked out of the gates along with her parents. Jasmine's mind drifted back to Niniya. She was now an eight-year-old who was attending classes at the Neuropsychiatric Learning Centre in Frankfurt.

'How I wish Niniya was going to a normal school like other children of her age,' Jasmine mused.

She thought of the fateful day in Bangalore, when things took a turn for the worse. It was a long time ago, but she could still vividly recall that one single instance of wrong doing at an erroneous time which now had such far reaching consequences. That's all it takes in reality. She had always been a gifted person, brilliant in academics and a source of inspiration for her peers and predecessors. But that fateful day, something had snapped. It was on a college excursion with friends. Few of them, including Jazz, had separated from the main group and had gone looking for some harmless excitement in the local market for what one of them had termed as an 'occasion celebration'. They found a peddler who supplied cocaine.

'Just one sniff in the spirit of companionship,' the friend had goaded her on, and she had succumbed.

It didn't worry them that it was illegal and could be highly addictive. Jazz didn't want to be seen as a spoilsport and played along in that moment of madness.

One sniff, and that was that!

Soon after returning to Bangalore, she wanted more of the magical drug until she became addicted. Gradually, her grades began to drop. She fell out with her true friends who tried their best to counsel her. By the time, her parents took note, Jasmine's fall from grace was practically complete. It mattered little to her that by then, she had made friends with anti-social elements clandestinely dealing in both drugs and illegal arms supply. She became their conduit in exchange for a meagre quantity of the banned substance.

A month later, she was forcibly bundled into a de-addiction centre on the outskirts of the city for rehabilitation. Soon, Jasmine emerged from there, chastened and unrecognisable even to her parents. Their misery, witnessing the phases of transformation of their angelic daughter from a victim of drug abuse, then onto a peddler for illegal arms and finally to the pale 'ghost-like' figure she had become, seemed like an eternity. Life had come full circle! Jasmine got another second chance at life, that is normally denied to most. She wasn't to know then, but her bygone actions would come back to haunt her again in motherhood. The good part, if one could call it that, was that she never had to tell Tobias about her dishonorable past. He simply wasn't interested. The strange predicament gave her additional guilt. It troubled her.

'What's the problem, Jazz?' her German colleague, Timo enquired. Jasmine glided back to the present and stared at him blankly.

'Nothing…,' Jasmine tried to brush his question aside and smiled.

'How's Niniya coming along?' Timo persisted. Niniya was a popular kid among Jasmine's co-workers and friends.

'Yeah fine, she's learning to look into the eyes of people while talking. When that happens, she'll seem like a normal kid,' Jasmine said.

'Oh, come on, Jazz!' Timo shot back, 'Niniya is a gifted child. Everyone knows that.' He recalled with wonder, 'I don't know how she manages to remember so many things so precisely. The moment she saw me last weekend, she said, you're my mom's friend, born on 19 June 1994. Your favourite colour is blue! I had only casually mentioned that in her presence, nearly two years ago.'

Jasmine giggled. 'She's also good at memorising mobile numbers Tim. Hundreds of them!'

'Seriously?'

'Yup, sometimes she can solve even complex equations which kids ten years senior to her find impossible! But then, they won't allow her to attend normal school.' Jasmine's face immediately displayed several lines of worry.

'Who cares!' Timo thundered. 'I mean…you watch, this kid is going to do something special one day to make us all proud.'

'Thanks Tim, that makes me feel better,' Jasmine acknowledged his sentence, with a show of some spontaneous 'fist bumping' with him. 'You know, simple things like responding normally to touch would help integrate her with others. The problem is, she doesn't like anyone apart from me and Tubs to cuddle or touch her.'

'It's a minor problem, Jazz.'

'I know,' Jasmine concurred. 'She's bereft of emotions and feelings, Tim, that's a big worry,' Jasmine said, softly.

'From what I researched, Jazz, autism isn't any form of diminished capacity. It's just that they feel shut off from the rest of the world, although everything does get through apparently. Only they are unable to decode it as good, bad or ugly. They're confused and frightened most of the time.'

'I'm too, for her,' Jasmine added.

Changing the topic, Timo asked about her husband, 'How's Tubby doing?'

Jasmine's face bloomed, 'He's rocking. Tubs is the thrust of my life who keeps me fired up! He says, Niniya should get the best out of this life. And together, we'll do everything possible to make that happen.'

'Amen,' Timo mumbled touching his heart, 'He's a good bloke, Jazz. That is...,' he paused, 'whenever he finds leisure beyond making millions of euros. It's been ages, since we last partied.'

Passengers of the Lufthansa flight from Chennai to Frankfurt began to slowly troop out to be greeted by excited squeals and hugs from their folks who had come to receive them.

'Ahh... Your friends from India are here, it seems. I'd better alert the others,' Timo said and hurried to the coffee shop in the lounge.

Jasmine's eyes remained focussed on the Arrivals gate. One of her childhood heroes, for whom she had the highest regard was about to emerge from there. From her university days, she'd researched and followed his work extensively. Stalwarts of Indian space programme like Vikram Sarabhai, Satish Dhawan, Dr Abdul Kalam and Dr Rangarajan with their pioneering contribution to space technology had inspired her to look at the stars, planets, the Moon in perspective. All in the 'elite list' except the last-mentioned scientist had passed away.

Dr Rangarajan was the first to show up followed by his entourage. Jasmine greeted him with the traditional *Vanakkam* in Tamil. The scientist beamed. He introduced the members of his delegation as they received bouquets individually to thunderous applause from the small reception committee. Cameras clicked pictures. As the head of the reception committee, Jasmine made sure she'd be the one to travel with Dr Rangarajan in a gleaming Mercedes Coupe. All other delegates got into their respective allotted cars.

'*Herzlich Willkommen nach Deutschland!*' Jasmine said to Dr Rangarajan in the car, which meant 'a hearty welcome to Germany'. He knew a bit of German and nodded with a sparkle in his eyes.

'Tamil sounded better though,' he said playfully. 'How do you know the language, Mrs Jasmine?'

'Sir, Jasmine would do,' she requested. 'My forefathers were originally from Tamil Nadu,' she said describing her family history. 'Along the way, someone in the chain decided to move to Bangalore. My mother can still speak fluent Tamil, sir.'

'Oh, nice.'

'Sir, we are now driving towards the Le Meridien Frankfurt in the City Centre area. That's where you'll be staying along with your delegation,' she mentioned while he surveyed the pristine environs of the metropolis and took a deep breath of the crisp Frankfurt air.

'Okay,' Dr Rangarajan smiled. 'So, what brought you to Germany?'

'Came here to study space technology, and got married to a German. Rest is history, sir,' Jasmine concluded with a flourish.

'Every once in a while, someone in the family keeps breaking the chain, I suppose,' he quipped.

Both laughed.

'Sir, I'm your local coordinator for the duration of this trip. Please note down my mobile number. You can call me at any time for anything you may need,' she said.

'That'll be an honour, send it to my phone, and I'll save it.'

'Sure, sir,' she responded and shared her number. 'It's very easy to remember for people from India, sir.'

'Really, how?' he asked.

'+49 is the code for all mobile phones here. The number that follows is 1215 081947. India got her independence at 1200 hours on 15 August of 1947.'

'Wow! Nice fancy number,' he remarked with an appreciative nod, adding, 'I'm impressed.' They rode in silence for a while.

'Sir, what's ISRO's future in space technology? Since we've distance to cover to your hotel, I'm taking the liberty to pick your brains. It's gold dust for me,' Jasmine said with reverence.

'Sure,' Dr Rangarajan responded enthusiastically. 'At the outset, I'm glad an NRI is asking me this question,' he began.

'The Indian space programme is making giant strides. Today, we are competing with foreign super powers. Many countries including America approach us to launch their own satellites since we've the capability to deliver with efficiency and more importantly, we are cost effective.'

'Great sir,' Jasmine clapped. 'This is possible because of great scientists like you; India is truly blessed,' she applauded.

'Thank you, but I am just a tiny cog in the wheel,' his modest reply displayed his genuine humility. 'My only concern is, politicians should leave us alone and allow us to do our work.' He fell silent abruptly. The childlike passion on display just moments ago, disappeared. A grim frown replaced it.

Jasmine remained quiet, respecting his privacy.

Half an hour later, they drove into Frankfurt's busy mid-afternoon traffic. 'Who else in your family is here?' he asked.

'I have an eight-year-old daughter, Niniya, sir?'

'Good, which grade is she in?'

Jasmine paused. She wondered if it would be appropriate to narrate her personal story.

'You can tell me what's on your mind,' he said, instinctively.

She described her daughter's medical history. He heard her intently with a grim exterior.

'You should take her to Sadhguru Jaggi Vasudev's Ashram, the ISHA Foundation in Coimbatore,' he suggested. 'I'm told he has special Yoga therapy sessions that helps heal neuropsychiatric issues in children. No harm in trying, isn't it? Of course, one must've faith in it for starters.'

'Thank you, sir, I do have faith in whatever India has to offer,' she replied.

'What I've learnt in my life is that when one is on the path of faith, one will be taken care of in every possible way. Faith is giving the divine a chance to act,' he affirmed wisely.

Jasmine understood that it was a moment of epiphany for her. She had heard the term cosmic synergy before but she was experiencing it for the first time. Its full import hit home hard at that very instant. She felt a warm glow pass through her like a divine blessing! A blessing that promised a new hope, a new dawn. The scientist for whom she had the greatest respect was now opening a new avenue for her daughter's cure and redemption. Overwhelmed by emotion, she held his hand and broke down. 'Thank you, sir,' she muttered amidst her cascading tears.

'You're most welcome, Jasmine, I'm sorry to have made you cry,' Dr Rangarajan said, taken aback by her response. He blessed her by touching her head gently.

'Not at all sir, on the contrary I can feel the benediction,' she said, still overcome with emotion.

'I've a contact person in the Ashram. You can get in touch with him quoting my reference. He'll help you with more information.'

'Sir, how can I repay you for this?' Jasmine asked, wiping her tears.

'Not at all,' he said. 'The easiest thing in life is to advise.'

His witty remark cheered her up, instantly.

'I shall start processing my Indian visa immediately.

Perhaps, Niniya and I can fly along with you at the end of this conference to Chennai.'

'Why not?' he said as he gave her a thumbs up sign.

'You know, it's actually a kind of technology working on the 'inner engineering' for well-being derived from the science of Yoga. Come to think of it, it is not far from space technology which is Outer Engineering!' They laughed together, their conversation giving a psychological thrust to the heavy ambiance for a lift off into orbit.

'Fascinating, sir,' Jasmine said in total awe.

5

Intelligence Bureau (IB) Headquarters, Delhi

Sharad Joshi, IB Officer, was at his desk in his office. He was in his forties and was passing through a midlife crisis. He was one of the IB's numerous undercover agents assigned with the task of gathering 'sensitive' information. They're, in layman's terms, anonymous, faceless people who keep their ear to the ground. Joshi hailed from Bhopal, Madhya Pradesh. His school-going teenage daughters believed their dad was working for the Indian Postal Service. So, did his parents. Only his wife knew the truth and kept it to herself.

His father's constant query whenever he visited home was always, 'Why don't you ask for a transfer to Bhopal? There's a post office here too!' His usual reply, 'I've been asking them, but they say no vacancy....'

The statutory rule was that secrecy of one's profession was primarily designed for the family's safety.

Joshi was aware that his job came with certain inherent

risks. During the initial days, he imagined himself to be a native James Bond with a loaded pistol tucked away in a hand bag. He even practiced the famous Bond line in front of the mirror, saying, 'The name is Joshi...Bond Joshi!'

He was a daredevil, an adventurer, taking active part in the risky operations in Maoist militant-infested areas. Over the years, age had considerably slowed him down making him more vulnerable. In his previous assignment, he had narrowly escaped death while coming under heavy gunfire. He was lucky to have dodged bullets and escape. One of his colleagues couldn't and succumbed on the spot. Joshi realised it could've been him! Every time something like that happened, he would tell himself, 'That's it! I quit'. Yet, the next day brought him back to work again.

He lived alone in Delhi in a rented flat provided by the Government of India while his wife looked after the ancestral home in Bhopal along with his old parents as Joshi was their only son.

The cause for Joshi's resentment was two-fold. The first, his father, in early December of the previous year had been diagnosed with non-Hodgkin lymphoma, a virulent form of blood cancer.' It was devastating news. The oncologist at Apollo Hospital told him that his dad had, at best, a year left to live. They couldn't go for invasive chemotherapy treatment considering his frail health.

'Let him live the next twelve months at home as peacefully as possible,' the doctor advised him in private. Joshi had to report for work at Delhi after a week.

General elections were round the corner. The Central Government had, through his boss, put the IB department under pressure for more ground reports. Joshi wanted to quit the job and be with his dad. Three months had passed since he last saw him. After all, it was but one lifetime, and he wasn't ready to let go of a parent yet. Joshi winced and leaned back in his chair as he heard his phone ring. It was his wife calling. He answered on the first ring with a racing heartbeat.

'How's he?'

'He's fine…for now,' she said. He could breathe only after that. 'He asks for you every now and then,' she said, sounding exhausted. 'I'm sorry I can't do this for long, Sharad. I can't lie to him that you'll be home soon. He's stopped trusting me.'

Joshi's eyes welled up.

'Are you there?' she asked. He mumbled something to suggest that he was online.

'All of us at home,' his wife explained, 'understand *Babuji*'s pain and try our best to comfort him. He wants nothing…but you!'

Joshi cried aloud. She felt guilty. 'I know how much you love him, Sharad. I understand your helplessness. Don't worry, God is great. Okay…tell me what did you have for lunch?' she asked in a faint attempt to divert his mind. He couldn't recall his lunch menu.

'Anyway, call whenever you feel like. I just want you to know that I'm very proud of you. You're doing great service to the country,' she said in a bid to pep him up before disconnecting.

Sharad got up and walked to his car. He drove thoughtfully. The culprit for the bottled up frustration and anger was his boss, Gurinder Bagga, a Sikh, the IB chief. Joshi had approached him a few days earlier with an ultimatum, 'Either you give me leave or I quit.'

'Oye Sharad yaaru!' the boss took off in his inimitable style, 'how can you even ask? Because of elections, my arse is on fire! You see for yourself,' he said lifting one leg just a little and with his fingers pointing toward his butt. There was no fire, not even smoke! But it was an obnoxious, revolting sight. Joshi held himself back patiently waiting. The boss changed his tack.

'*Mere sher,* Sharad,' he said in typical Punjabi lingo addressing him as 'Tiger' Sharad, 'you have a new assignment, as usual in disguise, undercover for a secret meeting of some *chutiya* politicians. Nobody knows what they're up to but top boss wants me to find out. *Puttar*, you're the best man I have. After this mission, you come back here and we will *aaram se* talk about your father, mother, *behen, billi, kutha* whoever.... *Theek hai*? And by the way, no shooting with guns here! Relax *yaar*....only cameras.' He had the gall to wink!

Joshi wondered if his family crisis was a joke to him. He marched out in disgust. '*Dekh yaar, bura mat maan na,* don't make it personal,' he remarked, as he left the room.

Joshi was always a loyal and honest worker. But the boss's attitude had tested him enough and he had reached the end of his tether. His indignation quickly grew to a disproportionate size. Suddenly, he felt something snap within. He decided right there and then that whatever intelligence he was going to gather risking his life, he wasn't going to let his boss have it! After the night of action, he reported back to Bagga, 'Sorry boss, they mostly spoke about chicken biryani, Bollywood starlets they wanted to screw and dispersed.' Bagga was left dumbfounded.

'Now for some revenge,' Sharad Joshi thought savagely. With a cynical smile, he unlocked the front door of his flat. Half an hour later, he was sitting in front of his laptop. With an in-built sophisticated software, it didn't take long for him to find the mobile number of Dr Rangarajan, the scientist at ISRO.

LATER AT night, he called the scientist from a phone that was untraceable. Dr Rangarajan had just concluded the first day of the conference in Frankfurt and had just returned to his room. He saw the private number flash on his phone display and answered.

'Dr Rangarajan,' the IB officer addressed him with respect.

'Who's this?'

'I just want to help you, sir, consider me a well-wisher.'

'Oh, a nameless well-wisher? I get a lot of these prank calls,' he replied ruefully.

'Details complicate matters, sir,' the IB man tried to explain. 'Anyway, I need to warn you that there are some very powerful people trying to harm you. I happen to know, so....'

Dr Rangarajan began to sense the genuineness of the person calling. He asked, 'Who are these 'some' people?'

'Well,' the IB officer wavered. 'Politicians, don't ask me for more....'

'Thanks for the useless piece of information, Mr Helpful. Actually, you've been anything but helpful,' Dr Rangarajan said, cutting him short. The conversation wasn't moving forward.

'Look,' Joshi tried to convince him. 'I...I've a video recording in my possession...that'll reveal everything, okay? Thought you'll be interested,' he said hesitatingly.

'What's in it?'

'These people met a few nights ago to discuss their strategy.... And all they spoke was about harming you.'

'Don't say anything more!' Dr Rangarajan stopped him. There was a note of curious anxiety in his voice.

'Okkaaayy...,' the IB man halted.

Dr Rangarajan was more than convinced. He couldn't believe this stroke of luck. 'Dear one, this is incredibly kind of you. Will you share the video with me?'

'But what'll you do with it?'

'These bastards are threatening me and my family. I could use it as an insurance to stay alive.'

'Okay,' Joshi said. Considering the pent-up anger he nursed against his own boss, he didn't need more goading.

'Does that mean you'll share the tape?' Dr Rangarajan asked, still unsure.

'Yes, but I will never testify in court or elsewhere.'

'Not required,' Dr Rangarajan responded excitedly. 'By any chance, are you in front of a computer?'

'Yes, but why?'

'Good,' Dr Rangarajan said. 'Is it possible for you to send me a test mail from an id that can't be backtracked to you?'

'I do that for a living!' the IB officer replied with pride in his voice.

'Great,' he said, 'drrang@isro.gov.in'

'In under twenty seconds,' the IB officer said proudly and pressed a few keys on his laptop.

'Got it,' Dr Rangarajan confirmed receipt. As a response, he sent a programme named Ganesh. A minute later a GIF of a *Playful Ganesh* popped out of the email and lodged itself as an icon on the IB officer's desktop.

'Did you send a GIF image of a dancing *Ganesh*? He's on my desktop now,' the intrigued IB officer retorted.

'Yes,' Dr Rangarajan confirmed. 'Please click on the icon, and it'll ask you for a password. You should type, "I'm ready to feed". You'll get an answer, "ok". Then upload your video. I'll be waiting online.'

The IB officer did as he was told. After loading the video, the playful *Ganesh* sat down on his bloated belly, acknowledging a receipt with a 'Bless you'. 'WOW!' the IB officer exulted.

'Now be ready with a pencil or pen,' Dr Rangarajan warned him. Seconds later, a 14-character digital auto generated code appeared on his screen, '**dR4/L9Gx\RV9W$**'.

He wrote it down quickly.

'It'll vanish in one minute. Be quick….'

'Done, sir,' the officer said. 'What next?'

'Good,' Dr Rangarajan said appreciatively. 'Just to let you know, had you missed, no one in the world, not excluding me or even the Gods, could've opened the file without the code!'

The IB officer had just received an invaluable lesson in transmitting secret files using sophisticated advanced technology. He was in awe. He realised the technology the scientist had adopted was light years ahead of anything he had seen thus far.

'Got it, sir,' he said. 'So, I send the 14-digit code to you?' he asked.

'No…no…no, you don't, sir!' Dr Rangarajan cried in alarm. 'It's too risky. Send it to a number I'm going to share with you on WhatsApp.'

'Okay,' he said. 'What do I do with the Ganesh on my desktop?'

'Email it back to me.'

'And later, I delete this copy of it on my computer?' he asked for clarification.

Dr Rangarajan laughed, 'Try…only if you find any trace of it! If you haven't noticed, let me say here that you're speaking with an IIT Kanpur graduate, officer,' he bragged.

'Huh?'

'See for yourself,' Dr Rangarajan said.

The IB officer guided the Ganesh icon to his email. He literally vanished into the mail without a trace. The programme didn't generate copies. It transferred as a one-and-only original!

The IB officer marveled at the ingenuity. His respect for the scientist instantly went up several notches: to reverence.

Moments later, Dr Rangarajan's computer received the well-fed icon of Ganesh. He sat securely on his desktop. As a last step, the scientist shared Sithara's number with the IB officer.

'I'll not ask whose number this is,' the IB officer said with a chuckle. 'It has been a privilege interacting with you, sir, I hope to meet you someday.'

'Thanks. Well, hopefully, not sir!' Dr Rangarajan replied.

'Jai Hind, sir,' Joshi retorted instinctively.

'Jai Hind,' Dr Rangarajan mumbled before hanging up.

The IB officer followed the last step verbatim. He sent the digital code to Sithara's number. Thereafter, he burnt the paper on which he had written the code with a lighter. Satisfied, he leaned back in his chair and lit a cigarette. He rarely smoked.

In Frankfurt, after a long thoughtful pause, Dr Rangarajan transferred the Ganesh to his phone. Automatically, it vanished from the laptop. Pleased with the fruitful work, Dr Rangarajan whistled under his breath and got up.

The phone call from the 'well-wisher,' had been a significant step forward although he hadn't yet seen the contents of the video. It was now safely lodged in his phone in a secure airwaves format which no one other than him could retrieve. Before he had left India, he had instructed Sithara not to delete anything that would land on her phone. She was the person who followed instructions. Of that, he was quite sure.

Seemingly, he wasn't any more in a vulnerable position. He could now set his own terms in dealing with the enemies of the nation. If the need arose, he could leverage the new information for an offensive stance.

'Bring it on, boys,' he addressed his imaginary adversaries, 'Ready to play your dirty games, but you'll have to wait until after 27 March, as some important business needs our attention,' he said aloud!

6

Le Meridien Hotel, Frankfurt

Eight-year-old Niniya Rosenbuch looked like an angel. It was as if she had descended from the heavens, perhaps as a subtle reminder to humanity that God had a sly side as well. He must've smirked when she was born, even as other humans wondered, if at all, why he had been so partial with her. Thin, frail and cherubic, with minimal but smart movements that were slow by normal standards, there were very few clues for a stranger to notice that she was affected by autism. Conceivably, she turned out so beautiful that her worried Creator decided to send her to earth—albeit by making her a little less perfect because of a neurodevelopmental disorder.

As she walked into the Le Meridien Hotel lobby holding her mother's hand with her golden blonde hair tied back neatly in a ponytail, it appeared as if she was making a public appearance at the behest of her innumerable fellow members of mankind. Some of her golden hair fell on her face just above her stunning blue eyes. The only giveaway were her blue eyes, that wandered aimlessly but, at the same time, trying to make sense of the strange world they found themselves in. Her eyes rarely locked their gaze on the person or thing opposite, with the exception of her parents on a few occasions and often of her favourite teacher, Frau Maren Eysel who was far more than just a speech therapist to Niniya.

Her favourite toy, a constant companion and her window of connection with the outside world was her mini iPad placed neatly in a designer handbag slung on her slender shoulder. It stored vital information for her to get through the daily travails of her life. Arranged in its desktop display were important files, 'my mother, my father, my house, my teacher' etc. The left out in the list all came under the category—'strangers'. Extraordinarily, Niniya was also blessed with an eidetic memory which enabled her to remember intricate numbers and characters that even a superhuman would find hard to fathom.

Dr Rangarajan met the mother-daughter duo in the lobby. Jasmine had insisted that the scientist should meet her.

'Hello Niniya,' he said bending down to her eye level and extending his hand for a handshake. She instantly hid behind her mother's skirt.

'Sorry sir, she's not comfortable touching anyone, especially strangers,' Jasmine apologised.

'Don't be sorry, Jasmine, it's fine,' Dr Rangarajan said. After they sat down on the sofa, he addressed her.

'Niniya, my name is Dr Rangarajan. I'm your mother's

friend.' Niniya's gaze was still on the massive chandelier that hung from the ceiling. She was always fascinated by dazzling lights.

'Look at him darling, he's your friend too and a great rocket scientist,' Jasmine urged her.

'Rocket?' Niniya repeated. '*Rrrrocckkeeettt*!' She liked the sound the word made.

'Yes, sweetie, rockets to the moon and planets,' Dr Rangarajan added. 'Can you give me your iPad for a moment; I'll show you videos of a rocket launch.'

Niniya hesitated. Jasmine prodded her, 'Give it to him, darling, it's okay.'

Her tiny hands handed it over to the scientist. He transferred rocket launch videos to the iPad using the Airdrop application and gave it back to her. 'Go home and watch them. When you come to India, I'll take you on a tour to the Launch Pads myself,' he promised her. She listened with rapt attention although seemingly focusing on a distant object.

'*Inndiyaa*,' the name escaped her lips. She leaned forward towards her mother and whispered something in her ears. Jasmine smiled.

'What is she saying?' he asked.

'She wants to know your date of birth! She's decided to include your name in her iPad.'

'Really?' Dr Rangarajan said happily. 'Darling, this is an honour. Thank you so much. I was born on 14 April 1969,' he told her. She typed in the date herself moving her tiny fingers on the screen. There was no stutter or hesitation in her movement. The two adults left her alone as she busied herself on her iPad.

'What an angel!' Dr Rangarajan remarked, 'God bless her. I think you should definitely bring her to India. Something tells me, it'll help her immensely.'

'Sir, my husband and I will be forever grateful for your love and understanding.'

Suddenly, Niniya murmured aloud, ever so slowly, 'Masters.... Department of Aerospace, Princeton University, USA.'

Dr Rangarajan was spellbound. She had googled him and was studying his biodata!

'14 April 1969,' she repeated to herself. 'Rocket science... USA...Princeton.'

'This angel is a genius,' Dr Rangarajan praised her in wonderment. 'Jasmine, now is a good time to take the ISHA Foundation man's contact number,' he said and fetched the details from his phone. She keyed the number into hers.

ON THE sidelines of the Indo-German talks for mutual cooperation in space technology and reaffirmation of the strong and growing alliance between the two nations, Dr Rangarajan had a one-on-one meeting with the head of the German space agency popularly known as DLR, Mr Johann Schmidt. He was tipped to be the consensus candidate for the next chief of the European Space Agency. DLR worked as a key partner with NASA and was assisting with their ambitious path to travel to Mars. Mr Schmidt reported directly to the German Chancellor.

Dr Rangarajan called his chairman on a satellite phone provided by the hosts.

'Ranga, give me the good news. What did Johann say?' Dr Bhansal asked anxiously.

'All well, chief,' Dr Rangarajan replied putting the chairman at ease straightaway.

'Aww…thank god; well done, Ranga,' Dr Bhansal beamed from ear to ear.

'So, I had a long chat with him. He was pleased to learn about our *Mission Antariksh*. He asked me to congratulate you on his behalf.'

'That fellow,' the chairman said, 'is a nice chap.'

'He was in awe, when I explained the objective of the mission. He said and I quote, "I wish Germany had such brilliant scientists like India has." He realised the enormity of the mission and gawked in disbelief at what he had just heard—"India will become only the fourth nation after USA, Russia and China to have ASAT capabilities!"' Dr Rangarajan echoed Johann's reaction!

'That's all fine, but get to the main part, *Ranga*,' Dr Anil said impatiently.

'Yes, yes,' Dr Rangarajan cleared his throat before the big revelation. He read from a copy of the statement, 'Germany stands with India in solidarity! Not only us but the entire European Union's support is with your space programme and the spectacular strides Indian scientists are making! We are all very proud of you,' he quoted Johann.

'Ranga, the nation is indeed proud of you,' Dr Bhansal's voice was sounding choked. 'Come back, now, I owe this one to you,' he said while wiping his tears of joy.

'Thank you, chief! But all this comes with a caveat, a condition,' Dr Rangarajan cautioned.

'Huh? What's that?' Dr Bhansal sighed.

'We should not be the first nation to use it in warfare. The 'Show of force' is fine for now, but an unwritten agreement that it'll only be a 'deterrent'. The role is clearly defined, as a defensive measure against an adversary's space-based nuclear weapons, a force multiplier for a nuclear first strike, a counter measure against an adversary's anti-ballistic missile defense, an asymmetric counter to a technologically superior adversary and a counter value weapon,' Dr Rangarajan reeled out the arrangement from memory.

'Fine, it's not as if tomorrow we are launching a missile with a nuclear warhead on our enemy!' Dr Bhansal remarked ruefully, 'but, will the big ma'am speak to our PM, when the time comes?'

'Johann was non-committal,' Dr Rangarajan regretted. 'He said he'll speak to her. He confirmed though that my meeting with her is out of the question, because it would send a wrong signal to the world. He wasn't sure how USA would receive the development. He wasn't bothered about the other two nations.'

'Hmmm,' Dr Bhansal considered, 'this was more or less expected, Ranga. A white man is always apprehensive of the optics and symbolism.'

'Absolutely! I thought so too,' Dr Rangarajan concurred.

'Well, fair enough. I'll take this gladly any day. I shall report this to the PMO at once. They'll be delighted, I'm sure,' Dr Bhansal supposed. 'You take care and come back safe,' he said to his star scientist.

'Thanks, see you soon, chief,' Dr Rangarajan said and ended the call.

WITH THE principle objective of the trip to Germany having been fulfilled spectacularly, Dr Rangarajan was feeling on top of the world. It was time to unwind. He was never into alcoholic drinks and would take just an occasional glass of wine on important social gatherings. He checked his watch. It was getting to be 8 pm in Frankfurt. He could possibly shop for his wife in a nearby mall and buy her a woollen jacket. She was always complaining of the inadequacy of her woolens for even Bangalore's mild winter! It was the scientist's way of celebration.

He called Jasmine from his mobile, 'Hello, sorry for disturbing you at this hour,' he apologised.

'Not at all, sir,' she replied. 'We don't call it a day here until midnight,' she said, making small talk. 'How may I assist you, sir?'

'Uhm...wanted to shop for my wife. Nothing much really. Which is the best place here?'

'Sure,' she said, 'nearest to your hotel is Skyline Plaza, a mall for things like textiles and gadgets. However, if you're looking for designer stores like Versace, then....'

'Jasmine dear, I'm a salaried man working as a servant to the Government of India. I cannot afford designer wear! Skyline Plaza sounds good enough.'

'Wonder how you can be so humble and simple, sir?' she exclaimed.

'We'll talk about that some other time. Thanks for the suggestion, bye,' he tried to hang up. It was very much in character for him to brush aside compliments.

'Sir, wait...wait,' she stopped him. 'Give me five minutes, I'll alert the driver. He'll bring the car to the foyer.'

'Hey! That's an official car for official business,' he reminded her. 'Tonight's jaunt is personal, please don't bother him. I'll find my way.'

'Sir, if you need anything, please don't hesitate to call me, I'll be up,' she said hurriedly.

'I will, thanks,' he said before disengaging.

Little did he know then that all hell would break loose, later that night!

It was exactly at 3.04 am, that Jasmine's husband Tobias woke her up. She had drifted into deep sleep and was completely oblivious to the world. She tried hard to get her bearings back.

'What happened?' she mumbled. He had never woken her at an ungodly hour before.

'Jazz darling,' Tobias said, sounding solemn. 'You need to come down with me; the… the police are here, honey,' he said gently, trying his best to remain calm.

'Police?' Jasmine sensed something terrible had happened. 'Is Niniya okay? Where's she?'

'Niniya is fine and asleep in her room,' Tobias reaffirmed.

'Anything serious?' She rubbed her eyes and slid out of bed, still confused.

'Just come with me,' said Tobias as he hurried her up. Jasmine put on a night gown and walked behind him to the ground floor. A few policemen in uniform were waiting. Outside in the foyer, she could see the fluorescent lights of police cars making colorful patterns on their glass windows. Her heart pounded with the thrust velocity of a rocket lifting off! 'What the hell has happened?' she thought to herself. She was getting a sinking feeling in the pit of her stomach.

One police officer addressed her directly, 'Are you Jasmine Rosenbuch?'

'Yes…yes, what…?'

'We've recovered a body tonight. We believe it is of a scientist from India, Dr *Raanraashaan*!' Even with the twisted pronunciation of the name, she knew whom he was referring to. She stared in disbelief. Her mouth turned dry. Suddenly, she felt her legs giving way. She was about to collapse, but somehow Tobias held her and guided her to a sofa. Someone thoughtfully handed her a glass of water.

'We need you to come with us to identify the body,' the officer said. It was all a blur.

'It can't be true. You're making a mistake. He spoke to me at 8 pm,' Jasmine screamed, agonised at this bizarre turn of events. She was so loud that it startled everyone in the room, including the officers waiting outside. She tried to speak, but no sound seemed to come from her throat. Her throat betrayed the brain's command.

'We're aware of that, Ms Rosenbuch,' the officer explained softly. 'It was the last call he made from his phone. Ma'am, we need to leave at once….'

'Give us a few moments, officer,' Tobias stepped in between the officer and Jasmine, 'I'll bring her.'

'Thank you, we'll be waiting,' he acknowledged and walked out through the door along with the others.

It was while getting ready in her bedroom, that Jasmine checked the missed calls list on her phone. There were 23 in total! The first missed call was at 1.36 am and the last at 2.55 am from three unknown numbers. Almost all had gone into the answering machine mode but there were no messages after the beep sound. Jasmine presumed they were from the police.

One missed call though, seemed an exception! The caller from an unknown number at two minutes past 1 am had waited online to leave a voice message. Jasmine closed the washroom door and listened wondering who could've tried talking to her at that hour. It was Dr Rangarajan!

'Jas..mine,' the voice gasped as if he was in deep distress

and pain, '*Niniya*... *Niniya*,' he repeated incoherently as if he was dreaming and then briefly stopped. He held his breath presumably having discovered something ominous, '*Sithara* in ISRO,' he whispered and fell silent following a 'bang,' a clear gunshot sound and running footsteps. One youngster's voice urged in German, 'Run....' With that, the line went dead.

BY THE time the Rosenbuchs arrived at the hospital, the news of the tragedy had been conveyed to ISRO and the PMO in India and also to the German Space Agency, DLR. Its shell-shocked officials huddled in a group outside the emergency ward of Frankfurt's Burger Hospital. Jasmine was ushered into the cold room immediately where the body was kept. The great Indian scientist lay motionless on a stretcher, bruised and battered. Blood clots from external injuries were all over the body, some prominent on the head and face. His shirt and trousers were torn and dirtied as if he had rolled in the mud in his last moments.

Jasmine, was suddenly unsteady on her feet. She covered her mouth in horror. Her husband held her firmly as she confirmed with a light nod of her head that it was indeed Dr Rangarajan.

'How did this happen?' Jasmine demanded to know after recovering from the trauma.

'Ma'am,' the police officer said to her, 'we don't know yet. At the moment, it looks like a hit and run case. He was found on the Mannheim-Stuttgart autobahn in the vicinity of a nightclub. He reeked of alcohol, so maybe he was drunk and....'

'He's a teetotaler, dammit!' Jasmine shouted, 'and certainly, he was not the night club kind of person.'

'Honey,' Tobias stepped up, 'they're only doing their job.'

'This whole thing is a terrible mistake,' she cried to her husband. 'Why don't you guys believe me?' she asked helplessly and wept. This time though, there was no stopping the tears that flowed from her eyes.

'I guided him to the Skyline Plaza mall next to his hotel. How did he end up in a night club in Mannheim, which is on the other end of town? Don't you all see it is absurd...!'

The policemen present in the room quietly made note of her deposition.

'By the way, where's the bullet wound?' she demanded. The policemen and the doctor were suddenly taken aback.

'What bullet wound? No one said he was shot, I checked, there's no such thing,' the doctor stammered, looking confused.

Jasmine checked herself in time. 'Then how did he die? Was it a heart attack?'

'He was apparently run over by a vehicle. We have already mentioned that. He suffered multiple fractures in the skull, ribs, legs, including internal bleeding. He must've had a haemorrhage,' the doctor explained. Traumatised by the graphic description, Jasmine fled from the room trying to keep herself from vomiting. Tobias ran after her.

It took a while for Jasmine to come to terms with the tragedy. The police waited around her patiently. Tobias shielded Jasmine, 'Last question, that's it. As you can see, she's very upset,' he pleaded to them.

The policemen agreed. 'Ms Rosenbuch, we recovered the deceased man's mobile. The last call made was to you at 8 pm. He also happened to send a text message, again the last, to an Indian number at 1.10 am, very likely just before he died.'

Jasmine stared in disbelief.

'We were wondering if you could help us,' the officer showed her Dr Rangarajan's damaged phone with a cracked display glass.

'Deal done! Inform Boss, amount to be credited shortly….'

Jasmine and Tobias, who was peering from above her shoulder, read the message twice. It didn't make any sense to her. She shrugged her shoulders indicating her helplessness.

'The preliminary enquiries show this number belongs to one of India's National Security Advisor in New Delhi working under their Prime Minister,' he mentioned casually.

'Look,' Jasmine exploded, 'It Could be the PM himself! I don't know,' she said dismissively. 'Or it could've been someone messaging from his phone after he died, right? The whole thing seems to be a set up.'

'That's possible of course,' the officer accepted the logic. 'Alternatively, he could've gone to the night club in Mannheim to meet someone secretly, finalised a deal and in the celebration that followed, he may've had too much to drink and unfortunately met with an accident.'

'This is bullshit!' Jasmine exclaimed. 'You're talking about one of India's finest scientists,' she reminded him. 'He was a teetotaler! I'm ready to say this, a thousand times.'

'Deal could be related to…rocket science for example!' the officer made a quick guess.

'Oh, come on!' Jasmine threw her hands up.

'I'm not saying that's a fact. It is plausible, that's all. Only further investigations will reveal the truth. Ms. Rosenbuch, do you suspect anyone?'

'None… sorry,' she said excluding herself from their wild, illogical speculations. 'I only met him three days ago. He seemed to me a thorough gentleman. Simple, humble and kind. Not at all the monster you're suggesting.'

'Right,' the officer said disappointed.

'A man of his prominence could've enemies,' she speculated aloud.

The officer signaled that he was done with the questioning, 'If you remember anything, please do share with me on this number,' he said handing her, his visiting card.

"The postmortem report will be ready by tomorrow. Our forensic team is already on the job,' he concluded.

ON HER way out of the hospital, Jasmine bumped into the Indian delegation members who had accompanied Dr Rangarajan. They waited anxiously outside the hospital. Some expressed their sympathies to her. A few of them were weeping.

'Can't believe this happening to him; he couldn't harm a fly' a delegation member lamented.

Jasmine told them about the conspiracy theories of the policemen.

'That is complete nonsense,' one member exploded, 'Sir never touched alcohol in his life. There's something fundamentally wrong in that assumption.'

'I know,' Jasmine concurred, 'It seems like a well-planned conspiracy.'

'Sir's wife, son and our chairman, Dr Anil Bhansal will be here by tomorrow morning,' one of them read a message aloud from his phone.

7

The next morning, India woke up to the tragic news of Dr Rangarajan's death with mixed responses. There was no official statement from the Government of India, except that, CBI sleuths had been immediately dispatched to Frankfurt to assist German police in the ongoing investigation. By evening, a mysterious audio tape had reached media houses in Delhi, purportedly in the scientist's voice. The conversation was repeatedly telecast on a loop by almost all the news channels with Dr Rangarajan's photo on one side and a shadowy outline of a stranger on the other.

The scientist allegedly asks, 'What's the deal for me?'

Shadowy figure: 'Quote your price.'

Scientist: 'This is explosive stuff. I want to hear your bid. Remember, I've to share it with a few higher ups in the chain.'

Shadowy figure: 'Would you like it in euros here in Germany?'

Scientist: 'Hmmm. Here or elsewhere, but surely outside India.'

The conversation faded away after that and was repeated again from the beginning.

It was enough fodder for the Opposition parties to join forces and throw up a host of conspiracy theories! The ISRO scientist was a traitor and had been found negotiating deals with unidentifiable strangers, selling India's secrets for an unknown sum running into billions of euros. The audio tape clearly states, they alleged, that he was to give a cut to people in the government hierarchy, a clear hint at the PMO! The PM, therefore, was an integral part of the conspiracy.

FOR DR Rangarajan's colleagues in ISRO, the news of the treachery was received with a sack load of salt. All of them were aware of the scientist's impeccable integrity. Yet, for fear of redressal, they preferred to remain silent. As a matter of fact, they were all given strict orders via official memo—'Do not talk or give statements to the press'. The scientist's abrupt exit was a huge setback for the future of the space programme in India.

For Sithara, the scientist's sudden death and the alleged fall from grace was a double whammy. She didn't believe an iota of it and dismissed it as a fabricated story. He wasn't anything like that. To accuse him of treason was equivalent to blasphemy! Personally, she was dismayed that 'misfortune' was following her like a shadow. She also had an additional issue to deal with. She had received a weird message from an unknown source that didn't make any sense to her. What was she supposed to do now that the scientist wouldn't be coming back? Maybe her future would remain a mystery, she fretted.

For IB officer Sharad Joshi, the whole issue was baffling. He was confused. Did the scientist really try to sell the video tape for making money? Did he err in his judgement of the scientist? He definitely didn't sound like a traitor! On the contrary, he came across as an honest individual and a patriot. Then, what the hell had happened in Germany? There was nothing he could do now. Fortunately, none would ever know that he had shared a sensitive video with the scientist. It could never be traced back to him; he was quite certain of that. Still, the mystery baffled him.

Newspaper headlines in every nook and corner of the country screamed, 'Traitor scientist caught in an underhand pact for PM,' 'ISRO Scientist & PM in a diabolical plan,' 'Mr PM, tell the nation the truth….'

Manikrao Kharmate and Rohit Sachdeva gave a joint press conference in the latter's party headquarters which was televised live.

Manikrao articulated in his opening remarks, 'The Opposition has an important role to play in strengthening the governance and to protect the institutional framework of the country. Democracy is not a one-party job. Here, our great democracy and the integrity of its highest office is under a cloud. In my political career, I've never seen a revered institution like ISRO tarnish its reputation colluding with a PM in this manner. The scientist had been caught selling the country's image and pride for a price at the behest of the PM…,' he ended with a flourish. The press lapped it up.

'Shame, shame,' Rohit Sachdeva cried dramatically. 'I've only one word to describe this, 'The PM is a thief!'

One party official announced to the journalists that the leaders would now take questions from them.

'Sir, who recorded the audio tape? Where was it done and why is it only for 58 seconds? Where's the rest of the conversation?'

Manikrao took the mike, 'At this point, we don't know the source of the audio tape. That's not at all important. No one denied the fact that the voice in the tape isn't that of the scientist. For me that means direct complicity. The government is deliberately hiding the facts,' he thundered.

Few journalists erupted with follow up questions but were silenced by Rohit again, 'Let the PM come forward and tell the nation the truth! I know he won't because he's involved in the theft of the country's assets. He's a coward.'

More murmurs. A member of the fourth estate put forth another question: 'What's the asset which you're alleging was stolen?'

'Like you, I'm also eager to know. Obviously, it's very valuable,' Rohit retorted.

'You mean, we don't know who stole what and why?'

'Look my friend, your PM knows everything. Why don't you ask him the same question?'

'...And until the facts are out in the public,' Manikrao took over, adding, 'we'll start nationwide protests.'

A voice from behind asked, 'Sir, who according to you killed the scientist and why?'

'I didn't!' Rohit retorted. 'You find out and tell me who did it.' Only a few people in the room sniggered at the pathetic joke.

'Sir, I didn't accuse you.'

'I know,' Rohit tried again. 'I was actually helping you with a headline for your newspaper.'

'Look,' Manikrao interrupted. He had had enough. 'We're not the investigating authority. That's for the law enforcement agencies to find out,' he added.

'Absolutely,' Rohit affirmed. 'Let them do their job. We'll do ours. We will not allow the Parliament to function until the entire scam is unveiled.' He made a last-ditch attempt to steal the thunder back from Manikrao.

THREE DAYS had passed since Dr Rangarajan's death. After the post mortem and completion of formalities, his mortal remains were duly sent back to India in a commercial flight, accompanied by his family. Instructions from New Delhi to the family came in the form of a request—complete the last rites of the scientist in his home town, Trichy. Kindly keep it a low-key affair. Consequently, only a handful were permitted to attend the cremation. An embargo on speaking in public or to the media remained. There was no condolence meet in his memory. Dr Rangarajan had been reduced to a mere statistic in an ill-fated list. He was another Indian scientist, snatched away by fate in his 50s after Homi Bhabha and Vikram Sarabhai, the two other scientists who had also died under suspicious circumstances. All three of them had endured mysterious happenings in their final days of life.

Jasmine spent a few days in solitude to regain her emotional composure from the trauma. She blamed herself squarely for letting Dr Rangarajan go alone to the shopping mall on that fateful night. If only she had insisted on accompanying him, maybe this wouldn't have happened. The conspiracy theories put afloat by the German police were downright 'preposterous' and cynical according to her. She had also heard about the bizarre situation in India where certain political parties opposing the current establishment were milking the issue for personal gains.

She hadn't revealed to anyone Dr Rangarajan's last voice message on her phone not even to her husband. She was certain somewhere hidden in those final words, lay a clue to the entire saga. Evidently, he was killed minutes after the desperate communication. Was he killed because of the message? And whose voices were those that could be heard in the background? Instinctively, she opened her iPhone and replayed it again. He had taken three names—Jasmine, Niniya twice and Sithara in that order, she noted. The last one came with a specification. Sithara was in ISRO! First, why did he repeat Niniya's name, twice? Was he hallucinating because he had been drugged? What did the little girl have to do with him anyway? Finally, who on earth was Sithara and how could she find out? Jasmine racked her brains for answers.

'Utterly mysterious,' she cried aloud and held her reeling head in despair.

As if on cue, Maren Eysel, Niniya's teacher and therapist walked in, 'Ma'am, there's something strange in this,' she said. She had Niniya's iPad in her hand.

'Is it about space launch videos?' Jasmine asked seeing the iPad in her hand.

'Huh,' Eysel retorted. 'No, it's not that. Actually, something else uploaded itself after that,' she said, showing her an image of Ganesh on the iPad's screen.

'What's this? Looks like a human with an elephant head, bizarre, isn't it,' Eysel remarked.

'It's one of the Hindu Gods in India, Maren,' Jasmine explained. 'But how did this image come in here?'

'I've no idea,' Eysel shrugged her shoulders. 'On the night you people came back from Le Meridien, Niniya showed me the space videos before I tucked her into bed. It wasn't there then.'

Jasmine clicked on the image vaguely. It blinked and asked for the password before settling back in its original place like a statue.

'Interesting,' she blurted. 'Are you sure you didn't see this earlier?'

'I'm positive,' Eysel affirmed categorically. 'I make it a point to check her iPad every night.'

'Okay, but why are you connecting it specifically to that

night? It could be spam also, isn't that so?'

'That's impossible,' Eysel countered, 'because we had consciously blocked all spam messages to Niniya's iPad. The Indian scientist was the first and last person to share videos on it. No one prior or after could've possibly sent anything to this device without my knowledge…,' she confirmed.

Jasmine processed the information thoughtfully.

'Shall I make a guess, ma'am?' Eysel asked. Jasmine waited for her to complete her sentence.

'I think it is him, the Indian scientist!' she claimed, with certainty. 'From the previous transfer of data, he could've sent another using the Wi-Fi anywhere. There's no other possibility,' she concluded.

'Please don't delete it,' Jasmine warned her. 'It could be important. We don't know yet.'

'Actually, I did try to delete it, ma'am, but couldn't. It just wouldn't go,' she said apologetically.

'Jesus, Maren!' Jasmine exclaimed. 'Thank god, for that.' She got up and paced restlessly in the room.

Concerned by Jasmine's anxiety, Eysel panicked. 'Is everything alright, ma'am?' she asked.

'Yes, yes, of course,' Jasmine dismissed her concerns. 'Maren, this is important. Can I trust you?'

'Sure ma'am,' Eysel assured her, 'anything for you and Niniya.'

'Please don't tell anyone about this, okay? Don't even mention it to my husband.'

'You've my word, ma'am.'

'Does Niniya know about this?'

'You mean this strange icon?' Eysel replied. 'Yes, she's the one who showed it to me.'

'Okay' Jasmine said with a plan taking shape in her mind. 'Can I keep this with me?'

'No way,' Eysel rejected the idea outright. 'Niniya will not be at peace even for a minute without it,' she said.

'Alright, give it back to her then. If she asks, say the scientist sent the 'God' for her protection. Meantime, let me figure out what to do.'

Eysel assured her and left the room along with the iPad. Jasmine was alone again with only her thoughts for company. So, Dr Rangarajan had shared a seemingly 'critical' file, presumably, just hours before his death, with or without his assassin's knowledge. One big piece in the jigsaw puzzle had just fallen in place! It became clearer that the scientist was trying to convey the exact thing in the voice message. That could be the only reason why he repeated Niniya's name. But, who had the password for this all-important image? Suddenly it struck her like a thunder bolt! It had to be Sithara, the third name the scientist had mentioned in the message.

'Holy Christ,' she spoke aloud, excited about her discovery.

THE FIRST thing CBI officers did upon arriving in Germany was to explain the facts about Dr Rangarajan's illustrious life and career to their German counterparts. 'He's one of India's leading lights with unimpeachable integrity and stature,' they had told the Germans. They requested that the investigation should progress in a free and fair manner, without any bias or prejudice. The late scientist deserved a chance to come clean; and they believed that he was.

'I've read the postmortem report in detail but would like you to read it aloud for all of us here,' the Indian CBI team leader Vikram said to the German investigator.

'Sure,' an officer volunteered. He opened the document and began to read, 'Time of death estimated to be between midnight and 1 am. Multiple graze wounds on anterior, posterior torso and limbs. Several contusions seen over the chest, abdomen and knees. Laceration of lungs and heart by fractured ribs. Automobile tire marks on the body and limbs. Fractured humerus due to injuries sustained as a result of being run over by vehicles at high speed. Importantly, a lacerated wound on the scalp and adjoining area including underneath it, in a distinct pattern, possibly made by a long, spiral object resulting in a fracture on the vertex of the skull. This particular wound is at a right angle to all the other injuries suffered due to impact with automobiles. It is not consistent with the injuries sustained by automobiles or their parts or anything otherwise found near the accident scene.'

'Is that all?' the chief of the German police asked.

'No sir, there's more,' the officer replied coolly. 'Around 600ml of brownish, watery alcoholic fluid with a 'fruity odour' was found in the stomach. There wasn't any trace of food. The time of death between alcohol consumption and accident was perhaps very less, at best say, 15 minutes, because its absorption in other organs of the body was barely 20 per cent.'

'What's the big deal? He drank and got run over on the autobahn immediately, looking for food!' the chief barked cryptically.

'Sir, please, there's more in the last paragraph. Symmetrical injuries found on the victim's wrists and ankles that could've been sustained while being pinned down forcibly,' he concluded.

'It's clear what you're implying, officer,' the chief roared. 'Any idiot can decipher that. But, my point is that the other facts are not corroborating it.'

'Yes, sir.'

The comments were met by a stony silence as others in the room silently processed the content of the report.

'Let's start at the very beginning, from 10 March, the day on which the delegation arrived here. We might've missed something,' Vikram suggested breaking the uneasy calm.

'They were met at the airport by Jasmine and her team and driven to Le Meridien hotel. The Indo-German conference went smoothly for three days. Nothing untoward. On 14 March, the fateful evening, Jasmine met the scientist in the lobby of the hotel with her eight-year-old daughter.'

'Any particular motive given for this meeting?'

'No, just personal we are informed.'

'Does the CCTV footage validate that?' Vikram asked.

'Yes, we checked. There was nothing unseemly, just casual banter,' the German investigator confirmed.

'Right, let's see it again.'

In the next few hours, they studied the video of the lobby

meeting recorded by 4 cameras. No fresh clue emerged.

'Okay, so what happened after that?' Vikram asked.

'The lady and her daughter left for their home. The scientist returned to his room. He emerged once again at 8.13 pm in normal attire and walked towards Skyline Plaza Mall, as claimed by Ms Jasmine Rosenbuch, where he went shopping for his wife, apparently,' the German investigator said.

'And that's where the trail goes cold!' Vikram commented regretfully.

'Yes, because his phone is abruptly switched off at 8.43 pm.'

The investigators exchanged blank looks and fell silent.

'Any theories?' the CBI's Vikram asked.

'He might've bumped into someone known to him and didn't want to leave a digital footprint of where they were heading and switched off the phone,' one of the German officers speculated.

'Could be possible,' Vikram agreed. 'Could be an unknown person too. The mysterious man or men or woman might've forced him to switch off his phone.'

'Yeah, might have,' another German opined, 'but what I want to know is, why on earth would anyone in Germany want to kill him? I mean, he's just a visitor here,' he shrugged his shoulders dismissively, in a manner that conveyed that he thought of the conspiracy and assault theories of murder by a local, to be bizarre.

'Sir, in India there are certain very powerful and influential people who could benefit by the scientist's silence. Because, in his capacity as a rocket scientist,' this man could possibly help swing public opinion any which way.'

'How's that possible? That's too contrived,' the German said, throwing his hands up in despair. 'So, you are claiming, that one among your country's powerful and mighty arranged a murder here?'

'I'm not claiming,' Vikram countered him. 'It's just speculation at this stage.' The temperature in the room shot up a few degrees.

'How far is the Mannheim night Club from the Skyline Mall?' One CBI officer asked diverting the topic.

'About 15 miles.'

'Can we check all public transport vehicles from Skyline to Mannheim after 8.30 pm?' the CBI man asked.

'The only available transport is a cab! There is no other way to get there.'

'Ah, ah, we've not yet ruled out the possibility of a mysterious man bumping into Dr Rangarajan and driving him away from Skyline Mall,' Vikram pointed out.

'That is if he existed,' the unhappy German countered. 'Hundreds of cars would've left Skyline Mall at that time,' he said, outlining the enormity of checking out this theory.

'Gentlemen,' Vikram addressed them, 'first and foremost, we need to study the CCTV footage of Le Meridien from 10 to 14 March from all angles, and all cameras to try and see if anyone was watching Dr Rangarajan. Second, the scientist travelled from Skyline to Mannheim using some form of transport. If we can establish a connection between the two places, then we're in business. Let's begin by questioning the hotel staff, particularly those serving guests in the lobby and restaurants.'

'Hard grind,' the German officer grumbled. 'Aren't we complicating a simple open and shut case?'

'No sir,' Vikram said to him. 'Nothing is simple when it comes to Indians!'

8

Jasmine by nature wasn't timid and submissive. When it mattered, she could be firm and decisive. She was capable of taking on any form of injustice, head on. She exerted herself to prove to the world that Dr Rangarajan was a victim of circumstances and not the perpetrator of a diabolical conspiracy against his own nation. In that battle, she realised that the enigmatic 'ISRO Sithara' character, was an important cog in the wheel. Sithara must be in possession of a clue to the mystery. Jasmine resolved to find her even if it meant traveling to India. But before that, she had to ascertain that the culprits of the grisly crime in Germany were brought to book. Surely, there was something they wanted to extract from the scientist. It wasn't an ordinary, everyday crime of mugging. It had a clear motive. Did they succeed or bump him off because of their inability to find it? That was the moot question. Understandably, they were dangerous people capable of going to any extent. She had to be careful.

After her mental analysis, she retrieved and called the number from which she had received the voice message on that ill-fated night. She held the receiver tight, waiting for someone to answer the call. After a few unsuccessful attempts, finally, a young girl, Jasmine presumed, did answer.

'He…llo,' she whispered.

'Listen carefully, sweetie,' Jasmine spoke, her voice, stern. 'I don't know who you are, and I've nothing to do with you. All I need is information….'

'Are you…a cop?' the girl asked in German.

'No, I'm not.'

'Then why should I talk to you?' the girl, trying to sound tough.

'Because, I know who you are and I can report and implicate you in a murder case,' Jasmine bluffed and waited, holding her breath. She had to play her ace card in the opening round, itself!

'I, I mean, my boyfriend and me have nothing to do with this,' she paused, presumably to consult someone who was with her, '…we didn't kill anyone.'

'Look, tell your boyfriend he has nothing to fear,' Jasmine heaved a big sigh of relief. It was working! 'Consider me your friend. Do not be afraid. I suggest you and your friend meet me at once. I want to hear your version of what happened that night. It's either that or an interrogation by tough policemen. Suit yourself,' she said, pressing home, her advantage.

The girl on the phone again conferred with her companion. She spoke after a long pause: 'We can meet you only in the evening. We cannot come during the day.'

'That's fine with me,' Jasmine punched the air in mock celebration adding, 'Meet me at 8 pm tonight inside the *Das Zimmer* nightclub.'

'We won't come inside the bar. There will be people. Anywhere else is okay,' the girl said vehemently.

'Okay, I will meet you outside the nightclub, then we'll walk to my car,' Jasmine said and disconnected.

She was pleased with the breakthrough but realised she hadn't asked the girl's name nor that of her boyfriend. It was inconsequential, she realised. It was a godsendthat they hadn't switched off their phone.

THAT NIGHT, Jasmine met the youngsters as planned outside the *Das Zimmer* Pub in Mannheim. They sat in her car nervously and claimed that they were innocent bystanders and had been unwittingly dragged into the messy affair.

'What did you see that night?' Jasmine asked the diffident boy.

'We were having a good time in the bar and after that, decided to return to our dorm around 1 am,' the girl answered for him.

'Why doesn't he talk?' Jasmine asked expecting him to respond.

'It's all her fault,' the boy burst out angrily, shifting the blame on her. 'I told her repeatedly to not go near that coloured guy. But no, she never listens to me,' he howled.

'It was just to help a man in distress,' the girl said, justifying her intentions.

'Okay, face the music now, bitch,' the boy scowled at her.

'Hey, hey!' Jasmine reminded them both of her presence. 'Calm down you two. What was the Indian guy doing when you saw him?'

'He was badly injured and bleeding,' the boy recalled. 'He was dragging himself away on the pedestrian overbridge across the autobahn.'

'Oh!'

'He wanted a phone to make a call to someone.'

'He was trying to reach me,' Jasmine said.

'I thought police...?'

'Then?' Jasmine nudged him to continue.

'Despite my protests, she gave him her phone,' the boy said and fell silent thoughtfully.

'What happened next? I don't have all night, dude!' Jasmine shouted impatiently. It startled both the youngsters.

'He...he could hardly dial the number, but managed to leave a voice message. Meantime, at the far end of the bridge, two men appeared out of nowhere. One of them fired at us,' the boy halted, recalling the nightmare. 'Fuck man, that was scary!' he shivered. Jasmine indicated to him to continue.

'We got scared. I snatched her phone from the man and ran without looking back. We thought they would come after us. For two days, we didn't come out of our dorm,' the boy narrated.

'I wanted to report the matter to the police but he didn't agree,' the girl added.

'Would you be able to recognise those men if you saw them again?'

'Sorry, no, ma'am. We don't want to. Please,' the girl pleaded.

'It all happened,' the boy interjected. 'It was dark and those men were far away anyway.'

Jasmine was convinced the youngsters were telling her the truth. She played the incident over and over again in her mind.

'One last favour kids, can you show me the crime scene?'

'Please, no!' the girl protested, 'You said we will only talk and then be able to leave!'

'Look, the man who died happened to be an eminent scientist from India and our guest in Germany. He deserves this much courtesy from us. And by some strange destiny, you're his only hope,' Jasmine tried to reason with them.

'Okay, let's do this and be done with it,' the boy said to Jasmine and led her down an alley.

Five minutes of brisk walking in silence brought them to an elevated foot overbridge for pedestrians over the busy Mannheim Stuttgart Highway, that lay a hundred feet below. Jasmine recalled the police officer describing the exact location where Dr Rangarajan's body was recovered. She was amazed by the location. It was a near perfect place for staging a murder and camouflaging it as an accident.

She noticed that both ends of the footbridge were dimly lit and under thick foliage. The boy and girl stopped at a particular point on the bridge, and said, 'He was here.'

Jasmine froze as if Dr Rangarajan still lay there asking for help.

'When he was talking on the phone, two guys emerged from that side. And one that shot at us, stood there. That's when I grabbed her phone and ran in this direction,' the boy said shakily, pointing towards the opposite direction. Returning to the place of action had rendered him wobbly with fear.

'We just retreated from the scene, as fast as we could,' the girl said, concluding her narration.

'Those guys didn't intend to harm you,' Jasmine said, trying to reassure them.

'Maybe, maybe not. We were shit scared,' the boy muttered, glancing around uneasily as if he expected the men to reappear again and start firing.

'Where was the guy who was pointing the gun?'

'I don't know, I didn't look, ma'am,' the boy cried helplessly.

'I asked because if we can recover the bullet, it will be crucial ballistic evidence that may help to nail the bastards,' Jasmine said.

'Fuck, fuck.'

'Calm down, Benny. It's okay,' the girl said to him patting his shoulder.

'This is a fucking nightmare,' he said, crying out in frustration. 'Trust me, I didn't look.'

'Can we leave now, please?' the girl begged.

'Fine,' Jasmine absentmindedly nodded, even as she was replaying the sequence of events in her mind. The boy and his girlfriend didn't need a second invitation and vanished in a jiffy. After they left, Jasmine went through the place inch by inch, with the torchlight on her phone. She didn't know what she was looking for, but after a painstaking search, she struck gold!

Stuck in the iron mesh in the middle of the foot overbridge was a bloodstained piece of cloth, presumably of Dr Rangarajan's shirt. The iron mesh was four feet high on either side. That meant no one could haul themselves up over the fence voluntarily or otherwise. The obvious conclusion was that the late scientist would've been bodily lifted and flung onto the highway below. He couldn't have climbed the iron mesh on his own, especially if he was drunk. It was close to impossible.

Jasmine took a picture of the piece of cloth on the iron mesh. She walked to the spot where the boy had claimed he was fired at and launched a search. Few minutes later, she found something that shone in the bright light. Nestled in the potted foliage was a tiny cartridge casing possibly of the bullet fired! She took another picture of its recovery place and sent both pictures to the chief of German police, sharing the google location.

She texted, 'Proof of innocence! Come and see for yourself,' and waited patiently on the bridge for the German cops to arrive.

THE CHIEF arrived with his a ballistic evidence collection team along with DNA specialists. They combed the area thoroughly. Later, Jasmine was called to the headquarters for giving a statement.

'Ms Jasmine from Bengaluru,' CBI sleuth Vikram greeted her, 'It's always a pleasure to meet an Indian on foreign soil. I've heard a lot about you since the time we landed here.'

'That's great,' Jasmine retorted confidently, 'Welcome to Germany.'

'Thank you, Ms Jasmine. I'm dying to know how you knew of this place, ma'am?'

'I came here on a hunch and looked around. The chief had mentioned the name of the highway where they had recovered the body,' she said casually.

'Well, well, like a Scotland Yard detective, huh?' Vikram said, a trifle sardonically.

'If it's a compliment, thanks.'

'It is,' he responded, turning serious. 'I meant, this particular place, ma'am, where you discovered the cartridge case.'

'Actually,' Jasmine decided to reveal the truth, 'Dr Rangarajan left a voice message that night, on my phone around 1 am approximately.'

Her revelation made Vikram and the rest of the German policemen stop dead in their tracks. Absolute silence prevailed. Their eyes bored holes into her.

'Why didn't you reveal this to us, before?' the German officer demanded, his voice visibly angry.

'Because, earlier, you were in no mood to listen!' Jasmine shot back.

Vikram interjected, 'Let her continue.' The German backed off.

'He was trying to say something but couldn't. Just mumbled incoherently. Then there was a gunshot in the background after which the line went dead,' Jasmine said.

'From whose phone was the voice message?' Vikram demanded.

'I don't know,' Jasmine replied. 'It said private number.'

The chief threw up his hands in despair, '*Gottes Will!*' he exclaimed. 'Stupid lady, they could be the killers! We could've caught them had you informed us on the night you came to identify the body.'

'They're just innocent students who were passing by. They requested, rather begged me for privacy. By the way, I did not know then!' Jasmine snapped at him. 'I came to know of the message only much later.' She shrugged as if to say, 'What's the big deal?'

'Ms Jasmine, please replay the voice message right now for us,' Vikram ordered her.

She knew it would come up sooner or later and was ready for it. She had made a copy of the voice message and transferred it to another instrument. The original had got deleted automatically as messages only remained for a fixed time frame.

'Unfortunately,' Jasmine kept a regretful exterior, 'it got deleted a few days ago.'

'What the fuck!' Vikram shrieked.

'You mean, there isn't a copy of it available now?' the chief asked in utter disbelief. He looked as if he was about to burst a blood vessel in his heart.

'I'm sorry, there isn't,' Jasmine said. 'But I've already told you what was in it, haven't I?'

The chief banged his fist on the table so hard that it disturbed the files and sent the papers on it flying in all directions. Vikram glared at her suspiciously with his hand on his mouth and with an incredulous expression on his face.

The chief swore aloud in a foreign language that none understood. The decibel levels rose with each word.

'You haven't been forthcoming and honest with us, Ms Rosenbuch,' the Chief told her bluntly much after he regained his composure. 'I'll have to treat you now as a suspect and arrest you!'

'Seriously?' Jasmine sounded surprised. 'You're forgetting it's me whs got you clinching new evidence.'

'Don't get me started!' the chief threatened her. 'I can turn the same evidence against you! Do you understand?'

Vikram gently restrained him.

'Why do you think he called you instead of police or his family or colleagues?' the chief demanded to know.

'I've no idea. Sorry,' Jasmine replied taken aback by his aggression. 'Guess, he trusted me more than the others, possibly. I don't know.'

'Don't worry, we'll find out,' the chief said. 'Keep us informed of your whereabouts from this moment onwards, Ms Rosenbuch. I'm also cautioning you, if something incriminating does turn up in this case, even remotely connected with you, I'll take you into custody for questioning,' he warned her explicitly.

Jasmine remained unfazed. 'Fine,' she said, 'This is, perhaps, the right moment to inform you that I'll be leaving for India with my daughter in the next few days.'

'India! Where the fuck in India?' Vikram said, startled. 'Sorry, why, if I may ask?'

'Personal reasons, but I'll still tell you,' Jasmine said, as she gathered herself. 'My daughter Niniya is an autistic child, officer. Dr Rangarajan had suggested I take her to the Isha Foundation in Coimbatore for possible healing through yoga.'

'Oh,' Vikram reacted sympathetically.

'I hope it isn't a problem.'

'Not at all,' Vikram spoke on everyone's behalf, 'I've been to the Isha Foundation, myself; it's an amazing place. I'll pray for your daughter to get better, ma'am,' he said, hands folded in prayer.

'Thanks,' she acknowledged gratefully.

'When are you leaving?' the chief wanted to know. Still smarting inside, he wasn't interested in this melodrama.

'Not sure, but sometime next week.'

'Do you plan to visit ISRO, Ms Jasmine?' Vikram put it across as gently as he could.

'I might,' Jasmine replied, slightly shaken, by his question. 'Why do you ask?'

Jasmine's discomfiture didn't escape Vikram's watchful eyes.

'My hunch!' he said flashing a wicked smile. 'It's also a great place. You must go there.'

JASMINE SHARED her travel documents for the India trip with her husband, Tobias.

'You didn't consult me before taking this big decision?' he asked visibly upset.

'The last few days, you know, have been absolutely crazy. I just didn't remember to tell you, that's all. It's for our Niniya dear,' she explained.

'I don't know how this…this Indian thing will help her. Frankly, I've no belief,' Tobias expressed his lack of faith.

'You never know, Tubby,' Jasmine said, firmly. 'Unless we try it out, how can we be sure it'll not help? And what's the worst that can happen? We'll come back anyway.'

'Going to India, isn't a small matter, honey,' he mumbled. 'And why now? The timing doesn't seem right. It'll be difficult for you to handle Niniya alone. Why can't the three of us go together after summer?' He was glad he had added the last sentence.

'Tubby,' Jasmine said, 'I'm going now with Niniya. That's final!'

'You've become so adamant,' Tobias groaned.

'Look darling, I was born and brought up in India. It's my motherland. You don't know the place as much as I do,' she explained. 'Had you visited India, even once as a tourist, I wouldn't have to convince you. India has an enigmatic soul that one has to experience personally. When they call it a functional anarchy the emphasis is wrongly placed on the word, anarchy. India lives, breathes and functions almost always on the basis of its inherent faith and beliefs. Trust me, I can handle everything.'

Not convinced by her eloquence, Tobias Rosenbuch chose to remain silent.

'Tubby darling, there is something mystical about Hindu Indian traditions and culture that's unfathomable. Even though I'm a Christian by birth, I believe in things like yoga and meditation because I've seen with my own eyes, miracles happening. And for good reason, from time immemorial, the world has been fascinated and attracted to her beliefs and faith. It might work for Niniya. Who knows? Medical and spiritual tourism in India flourishes on this principle. People have the misconception that it is due to the affordability of treatment options. Not at all…,' Jasmine said stressing her point. 'It is because they work wonders.'

'Fine, whatever,' said Tobias. He knew he wouldn't be able to change Jasmine's mind.

'Why only me, even the Indian scientist also felt the same,' Jasmine recalled.

'And yet he died after coming here,' Tobias muttered as a sour finishing touch. Jasmine confronted him with her hands on her hips.

A COUPLE of days after the Mannheim footbridge discovery, the investigating authorities got a breakthrough. The Le Meridien hotel CCTV footage showed a blonde white man in gold rimmed glasses tailing Dr Rangarajan wherever he went. The suspicious man waited in the lobby for hours together, ordering drinks from the lobby coffee shop. Even his rare trips to the restrooms were super quick. He seemed to be keeping a tab on all the movements of the scientist. The footage, however, couldn't capture a clear image of his face as such to identify him. Hotel staff who had served him beverages recalled that he spoke very little and generally conversed in English. The German police circulated the grainy images of his mug shot in the video and distributed them to their teams in the hope of finding out something more.

'Could he be our man with whom the scientist struck a deal in the night club?' the German Chief of Police conjectured.

'If that were to be true, then the scientist would've invited him to his room,' Vikram remarked sourly. 'Why take the trouble of going all the way to a night club at the other end of the city?'

'True,' the chief agreed. 'We shared the picture with that

Rosenbuch woman, but she doesn't know him. But she's a fucking liar and I don't trust her ,' he said scornfully, itching to arrest and subject her to tough interrogation.

'I understand your animosity, Chief,' Vikram said to him. 'Jasmine isn't a suspect yet but she is definitely hiding something from us.'

The chief scowled. Just then, two officers came rushing into the room.

'Sir, you're going to love this,' one of them said excitedly. 'We found the car of the suspect!'

'Huh!' The chief's eyes lit up like fire.

'What happened?' Vikram said, settling down into a chair to listen.

'We went through the CCTV footage of the hotel, the Skyline Plaza Mall and the Mannheim Highway,' the officer began. 'First, we compared vehicles that had come both to Le Meridian Hotel and the Skyline Plaza Mall. That gave us a list of about 15 cars for that period. Then we matched that data with the timeline of 10 March, the night of the incident around Mannheim. We narrowed down the list to one car, a black Volkswagen Golf Combi common to all three locations!'

'What's a combi?' Vikram asked.

'It's what you would call a station wagon,' the officer clarified.

'We have a passing shot, presumably, in the mall with the blonde man, gold rimmed glasses driving…,' the officer said proud of their meticulous research.

'Wonderful work,' Vikram clapped his hands in jubilation and got up. 'Let's arrest this man.'

'Not so simple,' the chief moaned. 'Sit down, please,' he commanded him.

'Why?'

'Continue officer,' the chief said, ignoring Vikram's impatience.

'The car with the number F – AS 1572 is registered with Europcar, the car rental service. Their address is Hanauer Land Strasse 334, Frankfurt 60314. We immediately sent our agent there to verify the details. Apparently, it was hired by a man with an Italian passport and driving license, with the name, Alex Giovanni. The photo matches with that of the man with the blonde hair seen in the hotel lobby.'

'What's the problem, then?' Vikram asked, intrigued by the revelation.

'We checked, it's a fake passport and driving license. It could be a fake name as well. And what's more, he must've sensed we're hot on his trail because this morning, he dropped off the car in Dortmund Hannöversche Str.107, 44143 and vanished.'

'Ridiculous!' Vikram burst out, 'How's that possible?'

'He could've gone anywhere, sir,' the officer tried to enlighten him, 'for instance, he could've taken a train from Dortmund to Amsterdam. Netherlands is close by, or even Paris.'

'Anyway, here's his picture,' he said, as he showed them a

colour passport picture of a handsome man in his early 30s with blonde hair and gold-rimmed glasses. All the men in the room came closer to have a look.

'What about DNA from the car?' the chief asked.

The officer looked dispirited. 'Bad luck, sir. The car has been hired by another customer and is in the Stuttgart area at this moment,' he disclosed sombrely.

'Never mind,' the chief said lifting his fellow officer's morale. 'We now have a clear image of the suspect. Circulate the picture to all neighbouring countries in Europe. We'll nail him soon,' he declared.

'Okay, sir,' the officer said and turned to leave.

'One other thing,' the chief said, 'do we have footage of him near a nightclub in Mannheim?'

'Unfortunately, no, sir,' the officer replied. 'We checked all the night clubs in the entire neighborhood. There isn't anything. We drew a blank. Neither the suspect, nor the victim were seen near any night club that night.'

'I see,' the chief pondered.

LATER THAT night, a blonde white man made an international call from someplace in the Netherlands to a contact in India. Their conversation was brief and to the point.

'Hello, it's me...my ID has been compromised,' he said softly.

'How?' the startled Indian on the line asked.

'I don't know, I think that the Indian woman with the loose screw kid blew the cover.'

'That's very unprofessional,' the Indian man sounded distraught. 'My leader would be very unhappy to hear this. He would've appreciated had you sent the woman on a holiday too.'

'Not possible, I had to leave in a hurry. Also, she's going to India.'

'Oh! That's good news,' the Indian man reacted optimistically, 'When?'

'Tomorrow morning.'

'Thanks…you take care…,' the Indian contact hung up. After the call, he removed the sim from his phone and destroyed it.

9

Jasmine and Niniya landed in Chennai by a Lufthansa flight. It wasn't for the first time that she was visiting the southern metropolis. She had been here as a child along with her family. For Niniya, the German citizen, it was a maiden visit to her mother's homeland. They checked into a star hotel chosen by Tobias. Jasmine had sent an email to the ISRO chairman seeking permission to visit the Satish Dhawan Space Centre. She mentioned that the late Dr Rangarajan had made a promise to Niniya.

'Sir, I look forward to the visit to the hallowed turf where the revered great men worked to put the Indian space programme on the world map. It would also be an opportunity to pay respects to the bereaved scientist's family,' she wrote. Jasmine's secret agenda, though, was to unearth the mysterious 'Sithara'. Armed with a pass to enter SHAR Complex, Jasmine and Niniya reached the coastal town that was about 90 Km away from Chennai.

They met the chairman in his office soon after their arrival. Dr Anil Bhansal looked rather subdued and sombre. After a formal conversation on ISRO and its future, Jasmine gathered her nerve and asked casually, 'Sir do you know a person here by the name, Sithara?'

'Who?'

'Sithara,' Jasmine repeated. The chairman looked puzzled.

'Never heard of that name,' he said, 'Why do you ask?'

'Nothing in particular, sir. Dr Rangarajan had mentioned that name during a conversation in Germany.'

'I've no idea,' the chairman said, looking uninterested. 'Look Ms… ,' he had forgotten Jasmine's name.

'Jasmine,' she reminded him.

'Ah, Jasmine! At this moment, ISRO and India are literally being roasted over hot, burning coals by unwarranted, wild conspiracy theories floated by certain political parties. Our PM is being unfairly battered for no fault of his. This is a very sensitive matter. No one in SHAR would like to acknowledge someone who is only distantly associated with my former colleague.'

She noticed he didn't take the name of Dr Rangarajan.

'I'm under tremendous stress and here you are from Germany, the origin of this whole dirty mess, wanting to know about some obscure person,' he said. He had already forgotten Sithara's name! He dramatically fell silent, picked up a glass of water and drank it slowly. His theatrics startled Niniya.

'I'm sorry, sir,' Jasmine apologised, 'but if it'll bring

you some comfort, the German police are gathering new evidence to prove that Dr… I mean, your former colleague was a victim of a diabolical plot,' she said quickly.

He glared at her wildly.

'Good,' he blurted out, softly. 'Great,if it's true. They had better do so quickly before irretrievable damage is done to this great institution,' he added, looking distant again. After a pause, he spoke on the intercom summoning his secretary.

An employee came in and stood at attention.

'Ms Jasmine,' the chairman introduced her to him.

'This gentleman will take you around the campus. Be my guest, and enjoy your day here. You can stay for the night in our guesthouse. If you need anything, kindly let me know.' It was an indirect signal asking her to leave the room so that he could resume his work!

Jasmine thanked him and left his office as she followed the man out of his room. He drove them to the launch pads in ISRO's official car, 'Private vehicles are not allowed in our campus, beyond a point,' he told her.

Niniya was far more fascinated by the miniature rockets on display in the museum than with the actual gigantic satellite launch vehicle pads. She quietly went through the literature for each launch vehicle model printed alongside.

Jasmine asked the man who was accompanying them about Sithara. He couldn't place her either or was he deliberately feigning ignorance? He suggested that she enquire in the residential colony for employees, 'Someone might have heard of this name there,' he said.

It was mid-afternoon by the time the launch pad tour was done. It was an exceptionally hot day. Niniya, not used to this tropical weather was visibly tired. She was already jetlagged after the long-haul flight. As guests of the chairman, the mother-daughter duo was allotted a premium guesthouse for their stay. Jasmine had Niniya eat her food, before she took a nap. She locked the guesthouse entrance from outside and set out by foot towards the colony. After walking some distance, she spotted some children playing in the open courtyard of a house. She walked towards them.

'Hey,' she greeted them, cheerfully. 'I need a favour, my young friends. If you help me, I'll give you all these chocolates,' she said, as she dangled a bag full that she had purchased from the duty free shop for Niniya. The trick worked. They immediately crowded around her.

'Does any of you know someone by the name of Sithara here?' she asked. The children looked at each other. One of them responded affirmatively, 'Sithara sister, the singer?' he asked.

'Yes,' Jasmine said, her heart fluttering. She knew nothing about Sithara. At least now she knew that Sithara was also a singer.

'She sings in the temple,' he said pointing the way to the shrine but eyeing the chocolate bag all the time.

'Thank you, darlings,' Jasmine said while distributing the chocolates amongst them.

After a fifteen-minute walk in the hot sun, she reached the

temple premises sweating profusely. It was locked! She saw a display board that mentioned the timings of the temple. The evening hours were 5 to 9 pm. Pleased with the development, she returned to the guesthouse and waited. Niniya was fast asleep. Jasmine moved to the drawing room and sat on the sofa watching TV. She switched on an English news channel.

An animated journalist facing the camera was reporting disruption of the budget session of Parliament by the Opposition parties demanding an impartial inquiry into the ISRO scandal. In the background, on the Parliament lawns, a few leaders with party members sat in protest. Their mouths were covered symbolically with a piece of black cloth signifying the 'stifling of voices'. They held placards, 'Open your mouth, Mr PM'! 'Murder of Democracy' and another read simply, 'Shame…shame'!

The journalists were chasing a leader who had just exited the protest site, 'Sir, what are the latest demands of your party?'

'We demand the resignation of the National Security Advisor and insist that he be charge-sheeted immediately. A Parliamentary Committee should be formed with members from all parties to enquire into the conspiracy in matters of national security. There can be no compromise,' he thundered.

'Sir, will your party allow passage of essential bills in the Parliament?' the journalist persisted even though the leader had by then got into his car and was ready to leave.

'Let the government agree to our demands, first,' he reiterated firmly before driving off.

The journalist concluded her report with a monologue. 'The opposition leaders are in no mood to let Parliament function. It looks like this session, too, will be a wash out.'

Following the impromptu interview, footage of members rushing to the Speaker's chair and the resulting ruckus was broadcast. A ticker message scrolled beneath, 'Budget session washout imminent.'

Jasmine hurriedly switched off the TV. All of a sudden, the room was suddenly peaceful.

JUST AFTER 5 pm, Jasmine went to the temple with Niniya. The priest was already present and getting the premises ready for the evening rituals. He was pleasantly surprised to see a young foreigner accompanied by her mother visiting his shrine! He briefly explained the traditional way of offering prayers.

Niniya's attention fell on the small Ganesh *murti* in one corner of the temple. 'Elephant God!' she yelled cheerfully pointing toward Ganesh.

'Yes, he is Ganesh, also the God of wisdom and remover of obstacles, dear,' the priest said to her in his native language.

'She doesn't understand Indian languages,' Jasmine informed the priest.

'Doesn't matter,' he said gently, smearing a small dot of holy ash on her forehead. 'Ganesha will bless her nonetheless with good health and prosperity.' Remarkably, Niniya didn't react adversely when the priest touched her forehead.

'I want to meet Sithara, a girl who sings here. Do you know where I can find her?' she asked casually.

'Sithara?' the priest responded immediately. 'She lives in Chennai now. You can meet her sister, Latha in A Block, Quarter number 41. She'll tell you everything about her whereabouts. Their house is just around the corner.' Jasmine felt as if the gods had opened the doors to heaven!

'Thank you so much, sir,' she acknowledged gratefully, folding her hands.

'Not me, you must thank only Him,' he said pointing to the deity of the shrine. They prayed once again and left.

Jasmine walked towards the quarters as directed. When she arrived at number 41, she realised her heart was panting madly. She rang the calling bell. A young girl opened the door.

'Hello,' Jasmine greeted her and introduced herself before stating the purpose of her visit briefly at the door. The young girl was Latha, Sithara's younger sister. She invited them to come in.

'Sithara is in Chennai now, staying in a working women's hostel. She doesn't carry a mobile. But, I can give you the hostel number,' Latha offered. She fetched water and said that her parents were not at home.

'Thank you,' Jasmine's face lit up. 'Can we call her from my phone?' she asked.

'Sure,' Latha said and dialed the hostel's landline number. She told the person on the line that she wanted to speak to the resident in room no 8. There was silence for a few minutes, while the warden went to check if Sithara was available. Jasmine memorised her room number even while her heart was beating so fast that it was threatening to burst. She could hardly breathe. Niniya sat quietly beside her.

'Dr Rangarajan sir liked her singing very much,' Latha said and blushed. Jasmine nodded in appreciation.

'Hello?' a woman's voice crackled on the phone after what seemed an eternity.

'Sithara, it's me,' Latha said. 'There's a lady here who's come from Germany! She wants to talk to you.' After a pause, she handed the phone back to Jasmine, 'Here, speak to her.'

'Hi Sithara,' Jasmine said nervously. 'My name is Jasmine. I was the coordinating officer with Dr Rangarajan during his visit there. I've something important to speak to you about. Can we meet, please?'

What she heard next completely flummoxed Jasmine.

'Ma'am,' Sithara addressed her urgently. 'Don't say a word more in front of my sister. Act casually and leave my house at once! Make sure you're alone and call me in about fifteen minutes on the same number. I'll be waiting,' she said clearly. She sounded calm and composed while giving the instructions.

Jasmine followed her directive, and thanked Latha while saying 'bye to her.

'What did she say? Is she coming here to meet you?'

'Yeaahhh,' Jasmine mumbled. 'She said she was busy and would call when she's free.'

'Oh okay,' Latha said, looking rather crestfallen. 'She's been away for so long now.'

Back in her guesthouse, Jasmine dialed the hostel number again. Sithara herself picked up the phone.

'Jasmine,' Sithara said, 'who are you? Why do you want to see me?'

'Because Dr Rangarajan asked me to. I know what happened to him in Germany.'

'Do you have proof?'

'I have, but….'

'Okay,' there was a momentary silence on Sithara's side. 'Please tell me about it now.'

'No, I can't; we have to meet.'

'Have you come alone?'

'No, I have my eight-year-old daughter with me.'

'Okay, where are you?'

'ISRO guesthouse.'

'Fine, I'll leave for ISRO from Chennai, right now. We can meet later tonight.'

'Sure, but I can also come to Chennai.'

'No, it's safer there. Can I stay with you, tonight?'

'Be my guest,' Jasmine replied without any hesitation. This was working out better than she had imagined.

'Will meet you in front of the temple at 10 pm. From there, we'll go to your guesthouse.'

'Looking forward to meeting you.'

After the call, Jasmine had time to ponder over

Sithara's remarkable presence of of mind and the maturity in her voice. Her demeanour had already left a favourable impression on Jasmine's mind.

JASMINE REACHED the temple premises much before 10 pm. She had left Niniya asleep in the guesthouse. It was dark and deserted in the area except for the isolated street lamps. She was aware that she was in one of the most heavily guarded fortresses in India. Personal safety was not her concern at the moment. Only the ambiance was eerie and therefore, unsettling. Suddenly, out of the darkness, Sithara abruptly emerged.

'You must be Jasmine,' she mumbled with a nod of her head. Jasmine studied Sithara. Brownish-coloured skin, short black hair held back in a ponytail, thin athletic frame, Sithara was clad in a traditional *salwar-kameez* and looked like a simple, average Indian woman. There was nothing flamboyant in her appearance, and yet, at the same time, she appeared elegant and dignified in the way she carried herself. Jasmine shook her hands. Sithara's hand felt cold and clammy.

'You've no idea how relieved I am to see you,' Jasmine said to her.

'Yeah?' Sithara answered. 'So where's the proof you spoke of?'

Jasmine had brought the recording of Dr Rangarajan's voice message with her.

'He left this on my phone, probably, just before he died,' she said and replayed the message.

Hearing the scientist's voice in his last, despairing moments saddened Sithara. Tears filled her eyes involuntarily. She abruptly collapsed on the pedestrian footpath and wept like a child, covering her face with both hands. Jasmine wasn't ready to handle this dramatic shift of emotions and didn't know how to comfort her. She sat beside her and slowly patted her on her shoulder. Sithara sobbed even more.

'My own father had literally thrown me out of the house, but sir showed me the way and asked me to pursue music,' she wailed.

'I'm sorry for your loss,' Jasmine expressed her genuine sympathy and extracted a tissue from her purse, which she handed over to Sithara. The girl took some time to compose herself.

'Who did this to him?' Sithara asked, her voice suddenly firm and steady. The determination in her voice was palpable. Grief had transformed into anger in a flash.

'I really don't know,' Jasmine confessed. 'Let's go to the guesthouse and talk.' They walked in silence together.

Back at her place, Jasmine narrated her side of the story in sequence. Sithara listened in rapt attention.

'Where's your daughter's iPad?' Sithara asked her.

'I'll get it' she said and went to the bedroom. Niniya was fast asleep. She could retrieve it from her bag without making noise and brought it to the drawing room. Together, they opened the *Ganesh* icon. It asked for a password, waited and returned to its original position.

Sithara recalled the text message she had received. She

quietly rummaged through her bag and extracted the phone that Dr Rangarajan had given her.

'Your sister said you don't have a mobile.'

'She's right,' Sithara replied. 'This one was given to me by sir for temporary use until he returned from Germany. Basically, it was to be used for a one-way communication, he had said. Even I'm unaware of its number.'

'That shouldn't be difficult to find out,' said Jasmine as she took the instrument from Sithara's hand and dialed her number from it. After a few seconds, the call landed on her phone as a private number!

'I told you.'

'That's weird,' Jasmine wondered aloud. 'Damn, there's definitely a reason for him to take your name after Niniya.'

'Here,' Sithara retrieved her phone back from her hand and held it up. 'This is the reason!' On the display was a coded text: **dR4/L9Gx\RV9W$.** 'This could be the password.'

'Where did you get this?' Jasmine asked, gaping. Her eyes almost popped out.

'Someone unknown sent it to me.'

'Wow! What are we waiting for, then? Let's try,' said Jasmine, literally jumping with excitement.

The two young women keyed in the password but the *Ganesh* icon failed to recognise it! They tried a few more times and gave up. At that instant, Niniya called out for her mom from the bedroom. Jasmine went in and came back a minute later with the little girl to the drawing room.

'Darling, say Hi to Sithara,' she told a weary Niniya

who immediately withdrew, uncomfortable in the presence of a stranger.

'Hello, Niniya,' Sithara waved to her. 'Oh my god!' she exclaimed and said to Jasmine, 'Are you aware that you have given birth to a *devata*? She looks as if she's descended from the heavens.'

'Thanks,' Jasmine blushed, 'she's a bit shy here.'

'And understandably so,' Sithara said. Both watched her take back the iPad and stare into it.

'She's as beautiful as a rainbow,' Sithara said completely fascinated by Niniya.

'You're the latest member of the Niniya Fan Club,' Jasmine declared.

'Is it?' Sithara cried aloud. Both laughed.

'I only wish at some point she'll be able to recognise emotions,' Jasmine's face turned serious.

'What does that mean?'

'Niniya, is an autistic kid and incapable of feeling or understanding emotions like normal people. She doesn't respond emotionally. She is either happy or sad, but cannot relate to fear, anger, or show surprise or disgust. She withdraws into a shell when touched by strangers and goes quiet.'

'Is there no medicine for this?' Sithara asked.

'Currently there is no medication that can cure the disorder or all of its symptoms. Back in Germany, she goes through therapy classes. Few drugs deal with a specific behavior in autism to reduce the tendency towards self-injury or aggression. But Niniya is truly a *devata* as you described.

Left to herself, she's fine and doesn't bother anyone.'

Jasmine's phone rang, disrupting their conversation. 'It's my husband!' she whispered, indicating to Sithara to be quiet.

Jasmine went to the bedroom with Niniya and spoke to Tobias on a video call.

Tobias Rosenbuch was surprised to learn that his wife and daughter were on the ISRO Campus.

'What are you up to?' he demanded. 'I thought you would be in the Foundation's Ashram by now.'

'Yeah, in a day or two, honey,' she answered. 'Just wanted to pass condolences to his family. I am feeling so involved with the scientist, as if a thread binds me and Niniya to him.'

'You're acting very strange since his death. I'm not having a good feeling about this,' he told her bluntly.

'Okay, just give me one more day, that's it. I'll call you from Coimbatore soon, Love you,' she said hurriedly before hanging up.

'Is everything alright?' Sithara asked her when she returned to the drawing room, lost in thought.

'Yeah… yeah no issues,' she said, brushing Sithara's concerns aside.

'What do you think the contents of the *Ganesh* file could be?' Sithara asked breaking the silence.

'Something critical is stored in that for sure, but we don't know how to unlock it.'

'So critical that sir lost his life in trying to protect it. There's one thing he did mention which I thought was odd,' Sithara said, adding to the intrigue.

'What's that?' Jasmine queried.

'He told me to remain cautious until 27 March. After that, everything will be fine, he kept saying. When I asked him the reason, he replied, it's better if you didn't know.'

'Could it be something related to the Ganesh icon on 27 March?'

Sithara shrugged.

'But we can't take this to the chairman. It's of no use, that much I've realised,' Jasmine wailed.

'Sir gave me ₹ 50,000 in cash before leaving for Germany. After I heard of his demise, initially I thought I'll meet the chairman and return the money but realised he may also, like others, further doubt sir's character. So, I have not done anything about it.'

'You did the right thing,' Jasmine acknowledged.

'Think of something he might've hinted at,' Sithara urged.

'You won't believe how many hours I've spent thinking about this. I am absolutely clueless.'

'There's one place though, where we could still find a clue,' Sithara said slowly.

'Where?'

'In sir's house!' she suggested, an idea had suddenly popped up in her mind. 'If we could look in his room....'

'A visit to his house is on my agenda,' Jasmine retorted eagerly. 'I could request for a peek into his study room.'

'Yes!' Sithara was suddenly excited. 'Take me along as Niniya's nurse.'

'Fine, let's do that tomorrow,' Jasmine agreed.

NEXT MORNING, they went to Dr Rangarajan's house on the pretext of expressing their condolences. ISRO management at the behest of the PMO had conveyed to the family to vacate the residential bungalow by the end of the month. Mrs Rangarajan along with her daughter-in-law and staff were busy packing. The scientist's son had returned to Bangalore only that morning to rejoin office.

'Did you come all the way from Germany for this?' Mrs Rangarajan asked, touched by Jasmine's gesture.

'No ma'am,' Jasmine respectfully replied, 'actually I'm here to take my daughter to the ISHA Foundation.'

'Lovely child,' the scientist's wife said looking at Niniya. 'He was fond of children and reveled in relating to them. He would say they're the future of the world,' she said with a touch of melancholy, briefly drifting into her world of grief.

They all sat in silence waiting for her to return to the present.

'I'm sorry,' Mrs Rangarajan apologised wiping her tears, 'would you like to have coffee?' she asked the guests.

'No ma'am, we're fine,' Jasmine replied. 'I've one request though, if you don't mind.'

'Yes, what is it?'

'Wanted to have a look at sir's study room. He was such an inspiration for my generation,' Jasmine waxed eloquent.

'Sure, you've come at the right time,' Mrs Rangarajan said, 'we were going to dismantle it by this evening. You see, I'm moving to Bangalore to live with my son.'

'Oh, okay, ma'am,' Jasmine said.

'How quickly things have changed,' Mrs Rangarajan lamented. 'You must visit my son's house in Bangalore. It's palatial, you know.'

'Sure, ma'am,' Jasmine replied patiently. 'Now can I?'

'Yes, yes,' she resurfaced again. 'They study is right there,' she said, pointing towards it. 'I'll join you in a while.'

Jasmine and Sithara got up immediately, not wanting to miss this chance.

Dr Rangarajan's study was typical of any scientist's workplace, a mix of order and chaos. There were files, books on rocket science, an English translation of the holy scripture, *Bhagavad Gita,* a picture of Guru Shankara, a crossword puzzle and more. Donning the walls were several framed portraits. One of them, prominently positioned was the President of India conferring the coveted Padma Shri title on the scientist. There was also a portrait of a young Dr Rangarajan as a student of IIT Kanpur with his batchmates and another portrait with his wife and his son's family. In the IIT portrait, the names of the students were printed below the portrait. Jasmine clicked a picture of the portrait on her mobile phone. A minute later, Ms Rangarajan walked in.

'He was very proud of being an IIT Kanpur alumnus,' she said seeing Jasmine admire the portrait.

'Great, ma'am,' Jasmine smiled. 'Was he in touch with his friends?'

'There wasn't a moment of rest in his life,' she observed. 'He was so obsessed with his work all the time. Occasionally, he would speak on the phone with one or two of them,' she told Jasmine and pointed at a person in the picture. 'Karan Sood. I think he's from Delhi,' she recalled.

As they were conversing, Sithara secretly clicked pictures of the pages in his visiting card holder.

'Ma'am, can I use your restroom?' Sithara asked casually.

'Of course, it's right behind there,' the host replied, pointing to a door. Instantly Jasmine drew her attention to another portrait.

'Ma'am, when was this taken?' she asked, pointing to another picture. Sithara had enough time to slip in a diary in her dress pocket and take it to the restroom.

'This was at a party after the successful launch of SLV 2.'

Mrs Rangarajan explained. 'He never touched alcohol in his life. Only soft drinks for him. At parties, he had his own unique way to avoid sipping alcohol,' she laughed.

Inside the restroom, Sithara took more pictures of phone numbers and contacts before replacing the diary back on the table.

Half an hour later, the trio bid goodbye to the scientist's wife and left. They were pleased to have gathered more than sufficient material from their research. Shortly afterwards, they vacated the guesthouse and departed for Chennai together.

10

In Germany, the investigators of Dr Rangarajan's case got a major breakthrough with the arrest of the blonde white man, the alleged killer, Alex Giovanni, by the Netherlands police and subsequently of his putative accomplice in France. Both were brought to Frankfurt for the German police to interrogate and chargesheet for the crimes committed in their country. Apparently, the Dutch and the French law enforcing officers did a favour to them by 'softening' up the suspects before dispatching them because, right from the moment they were brought in, they began to sing like canaries! They didn't need any more persuasion from the Germans. Preliminary tests were done to match DNA found on the scientist. A forensic analysis was used to correlate the weapon found on them with the bullet casing recovered from the scene of crime.

The chief of German police invited the Indian CBI officer Vikram to jointly interview the suspects. Both men got down to business at the police headquarters in Frankfurt.

'What's your real name?' the chief demanded.

'Benito.'

'Benito who?' the chief roared, giving him a tight slap as well. The handcuffed suspect recoiled with agony. His blonde hair fell back. Then, he slumped forward.

'Benito Lorenzo.'

'Good,' the chief appreciated. 'Had you mentioned your full name the first time, you could've saved me the effort of slapping you!' Saying that, he slapped him yet again.

'Why did you kill the Indian scientist?' Vikram asked him point blank.

'Look, this was not supposed to happen. My services were hired to....'

'By whom?'

'Some Indian guy,' he said casually. This time, the chief chose a blunt object to meet Benito's soft skin with force. It elicited a sickening noise and startled even a veteran at the game like Vikram. The suspect wailed in pain. They waited patiently for him to regain his poise.

'Seems to be effective,' Vikram said, admiringly.

'We can give you some when you're going back,' the chief gushed.

'I...I don't know his name, man...honestly...he...he came through some other reference. He only wanted us to bring this scientist guy to a house in Mannheim to talk to him. So, we confronted him in Skyline Plaza Mall at gun point and took him there according to the instructions.'

'When you cornered him at the Mall, did you confiscate his phone?' Vikram asked specifically.

'Not immediately,' Benito looked surprised, 'but when we were going down in the elevator, my partner noticed him fiddling with his phone. That's when we took it away,' he remembered.

'Write the address of the place you took him to,' the chief commanded curtly.

'I don't know…wait…wait,' he screamed hurriedly seeing the chief pick up the blunt object again. 'It's in the pocket diary your guys took.'

The chief summoned an officer and instructed him to retrieve the address and raid the house at once.

'Continue. What happened next?' Vikram asked.

'So, we handed him and his phone over to the person who opened the door.'

'To whom?'

'There was one guy. I swear, I don't know who he was. Later, we came to know he was some sort of IT expert who set up a video chat and also transferred data from the scientist's phone.'

'Then?'

'They had a chat on a video call and….'

'They?'

'An Indian guy in Delhi and the scientist we picked up from the Mall and the IT expert,' Benito explained quickly.

'Hear the next question properly, I will not repeat it,' Vikram said slowly emphasising every word. He leaned forward, paused for a second and asked, 'What did they chat about?'

Tension in the room suddenly shot up a few notches. The chief too moved closer in anticipation.

'I couldn't hear them,' Benito muttered acutely aware of what would happen next. The chief had had enough. He menacingly kicked his chair back and stood up. Benito was convinced that the chief was going to dig up his entrails with his bare hands and eat him alive!

'Believe me,' he wept like a child, 'I swear on God, I wasn't in the room. They asked us to wait outside.'

The chief and Vikram exchanged glances. There was utter silence in the room.

'Stop crying you fucking moron,' the chief screamed. Benito abruptly silenced himself. Benito had been expecting a blow from the chief and had cried out involuntarily.

'Next?' Vikram continued the questioning rather impatiently.

'We were called inside—me and my partner, and we were asked to search the man. We did. He had some recording device on him. We retrieved it and they made us hold it up so that it could be seen by the guy in Delhi. Then they told us to shift him to another room.'

'After that?'

'The Delhi guy called on my phone. He told me, there had been a change of plan because the meeting did not go well. So, we were asked to bump him off and make it look like an accident.'

'Then?'

'I objected because our initial agreement was only for bringing the man in. But he offered us double the amount.'

'So, what did you do?'

'First, we beat up the guy—really bad, man. We broke a few bones. Forced alcohol down his throat before that. Don't think he suffered much,' he said matter of factly.

Vikram looked at the chief sharply, 'May I?' he asked.

'Go ahead, be my guest,' the chief gave his consent.

Without provocation, Vikram grabbed Benito's ring finger and snapped it back so hard that it broke at its base and fell back loose.

Benito screamed in pain, almost having a cardiac arrest at the ghastly sight of his finger hanging limp from his palm.

'This is the return gift from India for daring to harm one of its citizens,' Vikram asserted. 'And unfortunately, we don't have any booze here for you to endure this pain. Do we?' he asked the chief who grunted his disapproval.

'You Indians are bloody generous!' he shouted, shaking his head. 'That's it? Only one? If I were you, I would've ripped off four, eaten two and taken the rest back as souvenirs to India.'

'Good idea, thanks. I might actually do that if he doesn't complete his fucking story in the next one minute. His clock starts now,' he said looking at his watch.

'We....took him to the foot overbridge and abandoned him there,' Benito continued, biting his teeth to endure the excruciating pain, 'I told him, "You are free to go now, cross the bridge, hire a cab and go back to your hotel,"' he paused to catch his breath. Vikram glanced at his watch impatiently.

'We let him alone for maybe two minutes on the bridge. In that time, we sent a specific message from his phone to a number as instructed by the Delhi guy. But our luck ran out and a couple of kids had gathered around him. We fired at them to scare them away. Then we put his phone in his trousers and threw him off the bridge. Later, we drove over him too...just to make sure that he was dead,' Benito concluded his bone-chilling narration. Then, he passed out, unable to bear the severe pain from his broken finger.

IN A Chennai hotel room, Jasmine and Sithara spread the material they had gathered from Dr Rangarajan's study. Niniya watched TV, with her gaze going off at a tangent. The volume button was at zero and yet she sat glued to the screen, watching the moving images.

'The answer to whatever we're looking for, lies hidden in this data,' Jasmine declared going through the photos she had clicked in the scientist's study room on her phone. She stopped at the picture of the IIT Kanpur students and recalled the name, Karan Sood, the friend of the scientist mentioned by Mrs Rangarajan.

'In the pictures of the visiting cards, is there anyone by the name, Karan Sood?' Jasmine asked.

Sithara took her time searching among the pictures from her phone. 'Yes!' she yelled with excitement. 'He works in

Infosys Delhi, 98101 XXXXX.'

'Great!' Jasmine responded and dialed the number from her phone. Karan answered almost immediately.

Jasmine introduced herself at first, briefed him on the events in Germany and then came to the main point.

'I got your number from Mrs Rangarajan. Sir, had sent me a voice message and I'm trying to make sense of it. I was wondering if you could help.'

'I don't know how useful I can be,' Karan expressed regret. 'But I'm truly indebted to you for clearing the air on the bizarre conspiracy theories. Thank you so much. Ranga wasn't like what they portrayed him to be. He was a true nationalist,' he reiterated.

'Yes sir, I thought so too and that's the reason why I'm here. If only I can do something to prove his innocence.'

'What exactly do you need from me?'

Jasmine told him about the mysterious *Ganesh* icon. 'Would you know anything about this?' she asked.

Her query was met with complete silence from the other end—it was almost as if Karan had gone off the line.

'Hello?'

'Yeah, yeah. One minute, let me think,' Karan muttered slowly. Minutes ticked by, the suspense building up.

'There's one classmate,' Karan thought hard. Parag Agarwal! he exclaimed. Jasmine could feel a sense of excitement.

'Parag was Ranga's partner for project study in IIT Kanpur. I vaguely recall both talking about an application similar to the one you're mentioning. That too in the days when computers were new! I'm sure Parag will be able to solve the riddle for you.'

'That's wonderful,' Jasmine cried, sounding overjoyed. 'Can you give me his number?'

'If my memory serves me right, he's working in Indore.'

'Where?'

'Indore, Madhya Pradesh,' he repeated. Let me find his number from one of my Whatsapp groups. Found it! His number is 98281 XXXXX.'

'One second,' Jasmine said, signaling to Sithara to get a pen. She noted down the number. So did Sithara.

'Thank you, sir,' she acknowledged gratefully.

'You're welcome. I'll give Parag a heads up and let him know that he should expect your call after fifteen minutes,' Karan confirmed and disconnected.

'Parag Agarwal from Indore is our man,' Jasmine rejoiced and looked at the IIT Kanpur batchmates' picture on her phone. 'There he is,'

Sithara came closer and peeked into the picture. A thin, tall man looked at the camera listlessly with a characteristic tilt of the head.

Ten minutes later, Karan called her back. 'I've briefed Parag about you. He works for Impetus Technologies, a reputed IT company in Indore. You can call him now,' he said to her.

'We did it, Sithara!' Jasmine gloated aloud. 'Impetus Technologies, Indore,' she said excitedly, before breaking into a spontaneous jig.

'Hey, let's call him first,' Sithara cautioned, bringing her feet back to the ground.

'Okay, okay,' Jasmine said and called him.

Parag Agarwal sounded sober and statesman like.

'Hello Jasmine,' he greeted her.

'Sir, what can you tell us about this Ganesh icon?'

'It's 'dgital encryption using secure shell", an ingenious method using advanced technology! Ranga and I developed this programme for transmitting secret files,' he divulged. 'It was our project work.'

'Oh wow,' Jasmine marveled. 'But what is in this file?'

'I don't know that,' Parag replied. 'There should be a 14-digit pre-generated password for this, without which, it can't be generated or opened.'

'Sir, I've something that looks like the password. He actually sent it through another person. It is…,' Jasmine was about to spell it out from Sithara's phone.

'Stop!' Parag screamed. 'Don't do that on an open phone line,' he warned.

'Okay,' Jasmine held herself back with difficulty.

'It's too risky. Look, can you come to Indore?'

'I can.'

'I'll unlock the file in front of you. If Ranga has used this technology to save a file, it means it is of critical importance. Something must've set him off.'

'Sure, sir,' Jasmine mumbled slowly.

'Listen, sister,' Parag Agarwal said, sounding like an elder brother, admonishing a younger sibling. 'You've got to be careful here. This is not like Germany. You're dealing with fire. There are people out there with crores in resources. I advise you not to scribble the password even on any sheet of paper. If possible, memorise it and delete the digital evidence. They can do anything for it….'

'Okay sir.'

'I don't mean to scare you, but be cautious. Call me when you reach Indore,' he said.

IN A matter of hours since the arrest of Benito Lorenzo and his accomplice, the DNA profile of both matched with that found on the mortal remains of Dr Rangarajan. The weapon they had used—a .22 Caliber gun that was seized from them, also matched with the bullet casings recovered from the site. Forensic evidence results from the lab had come back as positive. It was therefore confirmed, beyond any reasonable doubt that they were indeed the perpetrators of the crime.

'We've enough evidence to put them away for life,' beamed the chief.

'Any hope of extraditing these bastards to India?' asked Vikram.

'No idea, how politics works bro,' the police chief said, with a shrug of his shoulders.

'May be possible if our Prime Minister speaks to your Chancellor?' Vikram stated.

'Why do you want to take these scumbags? They'll spend the rest of their days in a prison here, in case they happen to escape the lethal injection by court order,' the chief assured.

'Hmmm,' Vikram nodded. 'Anyway, it's not our problem.'

'There's one issue though, that needs your immediate consideration, Mr Vikram,' the chief said. 'Benito's accomplice has confessed that he warned the Delhi guy about Ms Jasmine Rosenbuch and her daughter's visit to India.'

'Oh...that's serious!' Vikram cried out in alarm.

'Now, it is pretty much clear that the scientist somehow hoodwinked all of us and managed to send some data to her. And she on her part, fancies herself to be some sort of a superwoman,' probably the next saviour of the world, even at the risk of putting her own daughter's life in danger,' the chief said, his words laced with sarcasm.

'That's true,' Vikram agreed.

'Mr Vikram,' the chief addressed him, 'the investigation here is all but wrapped up. You must return to India at once and save this headstrong, stupid woman's life. She could be in for some serious harm, my friend,' the chief speculated.

'Can we at least caution her?' Vikram asked.

'She might panic, unnecessarily,' the chief said. 'Let me talk to her husband and find out where she is.' He dialed Tobias Rosenbuch.

'Good evening, Mr Rosenbuch,' the chief greeted after identifying himself. 'I've some good news for you. We've apprehended the murderers of the Indian scientist,' he announced proudly.

'Yes, yes, it wasn't an accident,' he continued. 'They are European contract killers hired by someone from India.

We believe it is part of a larger international conspiracy. Investigations are still underway. Just wanted to share this happy update with your wife. Hope she's enjoying her India visit?'

'Wonderful to hear, chief, and congratulations!' Tobias complimented. 'Yes, Jasmine is fine and having a good time. I'll convey the news to her.'

'Which part of India is she in, right now?' the chief queried offhandedly.

'I spoke to her this morning. She was in ISRO to pay her condolences to the scientist's family.'

'Oh ISRO!' he said aloud for Vikram's sake, who flashed him a thumbs up sign. 'So nice. Alright, say cheers to her from all of us here, bye.' He disconnected and grunted. 'Damn, this woman never gives up….'

'So long as she's in ISRO, she's safe,' Vikram said slowly.

'We've the mobile number of this Delhi man. Wouldn't it help to nab him,' the chief asked.

'Don't be so naïve, chief,' Vikram replied, 'a man who's planned a murder right under your nose here in Germany, from India! Would he be so stupid as to hang on to that number?'

The chief glared at him and slipped into deep thought.

'IT'S A gentle warning for us to be careful, Jasmine,' Sithara said after Parag Agarwal's call. 'It's not a secret anymore that you're here from Germany digging into the motives for sir's murder.'

'Alright,' Jasmine said. 'So how do we go about it? It's not as if we are doing anything wrong.'

'You're doing absolutely right and I'm with you,' Sithara assured her in solidarity. 'Only we need to be smart here and watch our backs at every step.'

'First step, show Niniya the password on your phone. She'll memorise it,' Jasmine said.

'What? really?' Sithara was dumbfounded.

'Yes, she's blessed with an extraordinary memory.'

Jasmine took the phone and placed the password display in front of Niniya, who stared at it for a few seconds and looked away.

'That's it, the password is secure in her memory,' Jasmine said returning the phone.

'I can't believe this,' Sithara said in awe.

'We'll ask her two days later, she'll write it down for us. Okay, what next?'

'For starters, we need to move out of this hotel and maintain a low profile. Have you given them my ID for tonight's stay?' Sithara enquired.

'No, not.'

'Good, let's check out from here.'

'And go where?'

Sithara thought for a moment. 'If you don't mind, you can stay with me in my hostel dormitory. No one will ask for names or ID there. We've to just pay ₹500, but it won't be like here.'

'That's not a problem,' Jasmine replied. 'I've stayed in worse joints.'

'It's not much, but surely safe. In any case, it's just a question of one night. We're leaving for Indore tomorrow,' Sithara reminded her.

'If you feel it's the right way, then let's do it,' Jasmine conceded.

'I've one more suggestion,' said Sithara.

Jasmine looked at her, expectantly.

'Niniya is a sitting duck with her golden blonde hair…a perfect giveaway.'

'No way! I will not let it be chopped off! Tubby will kill me,' she protested.

'No, ma'am,' Sithara said, 'not chopping, just colouring. I was going to say dye the hair black like any Indian girl. We'll even put a red *bindi* on her forehead! No one will be able to recognise her. In two to three weeks, her hair will become 'golden' again.'

'Aren't you over-reacting? I mean, is all this really necessary?' Jasmine questioned, sounding confused.

'Sister, it is better to be cautious now than to be sorry later.'

'Stop talking like Parag Agarwal now.'

Both chuckled.

'There's a salon called Green Trends close by. I'll take Niniya there with me and be back in an hour. Meantime, you explore how we can travel to Indore on the net. Also inform the reception that you're checking out,' Sithara spelled out a plan.

'That's sweet. Take my wallet with you,' Jasmine said and got her daughter ready to step out.

'No, thanks,' Sithara replied. 'I have mine.'

'Thanks,' she acknowledged. 'I'm going to miss her golden locks,' she said ruefully, feeling her daughter's silky hair.

'Hello, they aren't going anywhere, sister. Stop behaving like her,' Sithara said. Both of them laughed together.

'Sweetheart, do you need your iPad now? Can't we leave it here,' Sithara gently asked Niniya gesturing at the door with her hands.

Jasmine laughed, 'She isn't going anywhere without that.'

'Alright, you can keep it,' Sithara said to Niniya. 'Say bye to mummy.'

Niniya stood still.

'Fine, let's go then,' Sithara led her away.

A TALL, muscular man entered the hotel furtively through the service entrance meant for drivers and staff, minutes after Sithara had left with Niniya. He walked purposefully to the guest elevator and rode up to the eighth floor. He knocked gently on the door of Room no 805.

'Evening service, ma'am,' he whispered gently.

Jasmine opened the door, spontaneously, without suspicion. She noticed that he looked anything but housekeeping staff. Before she could react, he pushed her back and entered the room, closing the door behind him, all in one swift motion.

'Who are you?' she asked paralysed by the speed with which it all happened.

In response, the man pulled out a plastic cover from his bag and shoved it over her head. He pushed her on to the bed violently and held her captive for almost a minute, before suddenly releasing her. Jasmine rolled over and fell awkwardly between the bed and the sofa, gasping for breath. He came closer and whispered in her ear.

'Where's the video?'

'What vi…?' the words seemed stuck in her mouth.

He didn't give her another second chance. He again choked her face with the plastic bag and held it longer over her head, this time.

'I won't ask again and again. Where's the video?' he said pinning her down with the weight of his body over hers.

'I don't know what you are talking about.'

He studied her for a full minute. She lay trapped beneath him, waiting for the unexpected. Third time wasn't lucky for Jasmine. He pulled the plastic cover once again over her head for one final time and savagely cut her oxygen supply. Jasmine lost consciousness.

Leaving her on the floor, the man got to work. He removed a nylon rope from his bag and tied her hands behind, all the while whistling under his breath. This was his favourite part. He loved snuffing out human lives. On the previous occasion, in ISRO, knowing his fetish, his boss had clearly instructed him not to kill the scientist.

'It's only to instil fear, Bheekar, just like your name. To scare!'

Today though, it was a no-holds barred assignment and he was loving it. He folded a bedsheet in the middle turning it into a long cord. He flung one end of it over the fan and tested its strength. Satisfied, he expertly made a noose with the other end of the bedsheet. He fitted Jasmine's neck in the noose and hoisted up her limp body. She squirmed a bit, struggling for few seconds like a fish struggles for life when put out of the water. Bheekar held her steady until the last remnants of life left her frame. He let go of her and swiftly untied her hands. Jasmine rotated in a semi-circle with the disturbance and finally returned to a motionless state.

Thereafter, he searched the room thoroughly. He put her phone and laptop into his bag along with the lethal plastic cover and nylon rope. He checked the wardrobes, washroom, balcony and security locker and suitcase. Nothing interested him. He meticulously wiped the place clean making sure there were no fingerprints. Satisfied with his work, he glanced at Jasmine. She seemed at peace with herself in death. He stood still and crossed his heart. Finally, Bheekar removed a suicide note from his bag. Two lines were typed neatly on the hotel's letterhead. He carefully placed it on the table.

'*This is the only way for me to relieve Niniya's miserable condition.... Sorry, Tubby.*'

He surveyed the room. It was exactly like what it had been before he had arrived. Satisfied by his ingenuity, Bheekar left the room, closing the door softly behind him. With eyes on the floor ahead, he walked quickly to the elevator and rode down to the lobby. He reached his car, flung the bag on to the rear seat and gave a missed-call to someone. It had been fun, he supposed, smiling diabolically to himself.

The recipient of the missed call looked at his watch and proceeded to push a few buttons on the keypad of the computer in front of him. It immediately identified the fault in the CCTV camera's operation that had been shut down for repairs since an hour. He called his technical team on the intercom.

'Problem identified, guys. It seems like the usual cable fault due to rodents. Please return to the server room in the basement. We need to fix this as soon as possible,' he informed them. The relieved technicians trooped into the server room and got down to work.

11

He was the invisible assassin for his boss. His work was typically covert. His existence was rarely known beyond that close, inner circle. Apart from his employer, only a few others knew his actual name, Bheekar, the fearful one. Stories of his ruthlessness were legendary and he was always spoken about in hushed tones! Pushing the reclining seat further back in the car, Bheekar called his employer. He sounded unusually happy and peaceful.

'Sir, the lady has been sent on a long vacation,' he reported. 'Sadly, she forgot to take her phone and laptop. I checked them for any forwarding address or phone numbers, but there weren't any.'

'Hmmm,' the boss grimaced. 'Did you ask her about tape recording places of interest?'

'Yes, sir, she wasn't aware of any. I checked her bags too and found nothing.'

'Hmmm,' the employer, Manikrao Kharmate pondered over it. 'My initial hunch was right. This whole claim of having tapes is a hoax. I don't think we should waste our time anymore on this. Whom did she call anyway?'

'I scanned the call list through my True Caller ID. A couple of IT guys in Delhi and Indore, that's all. Also, some pictures clicked in our friend's house…,' he stated.

'She was also possibly searching in the dark like us!' Kharmate sniggered. 'By the way, where's her little girl?'

'She wasn't there,' Bheekar said mournfully. 'I was planning to send her along with the mother.'

'You and your bloody obsession!' Kharmate cried out in mock horror. 'Sometimes, I feel you did not grow up at all.'

'Sir, what should I do now?'

'What do you mean? I can't make you grow up!'

'Sir.'

Kharmate smiled to himself. 'Is the news about the lady out in the public domain?' he asked in return.

'Not yet, sir.'

'Well, inform them. Hang around in the vicinity for some time. Who knows, the little girl may reappear so, you may still have a chance to have some more fun. Or else, you can come back.'

'Fine, sir,' Bheekar said. He seemed to be relishing the idea of waiting for the little girl to come back.

'And remind me later,' Kharmate said, 'to thank our good friend Senthil for his logistics support.'

'Will do, sir.'

SITHARA ALONG with Niniya in a new incarnation as a fair, little Indian girl with flowing black hair strolled towards their hotel. Her transformation from a European to a subcontinent native was remarkable. Sithara had added a regal red *bindi* on her forehead to make her practically unrecognisable. As they passed the gate and entered the hotel premises, Sithara overheard a man from a parked car, mention a room number and this instantly caught her attention. Only a row of potted plants separated her from him. She stayed still, holding back Niniya.

'Yes, Room 805. I've been trying to reach her, but she's not answering. Something might've happened. Could you send someone to check please.'

The man, oddly, didn't seem to be disconcerted and didn't appear concerned. On the contrary, he began to whistle a tune immediately after the call. Sithara could immediately sense that something terrible had happened to Jasmine. She instinctively clicked pictures of the man on her phone through the camouflage of the green foliage. She managed to capture clear shots of his face and profile. Quickening her pace, she reached the lobby and scouted for a secure place where she could leave Niniya. It was a risky option, but there wasn't any other. She found a secluded spot and helped Niniya on to a sofa, lifting her and thrusting a magazine in her hand.

'Don't move from here until I come back,' she instructed the little girl. She wasn't sure how much the kid understood as her gaze, as usual, was wandering elsewhere. Niniya, on her part began to silently examine the pages of the journal in her hand.

As it was, it was a wonder that Niniya had not run away from Sithara and had allowed her to hold her hand. Earlier, even Jasmine had been surprised that she had happily trotted along with Sithara for the hair colouring experiment. Jasmine had recalled that back in the temple at ISRO, Niniya had not recoiled when the priest had applied holy paste on her forehead. That too, had surprised Jasmine. Was it something to do with being in India, an ancient spiritual land?

Leaving her alone, Sithara resolutely walked towards the elevators. Managerial staff along with a security officer were already waiting for the next elevator.

'Tried from the reception. No response,' the manager said to the security-in-charge.

'She might be asleep.'

'Hope so.'

'What's the name of the guest?'

'Some Jasmine from Germany.'

Sithara felt as if she had been struck by lightning. She quietly got into the elevator with them. They remained silent as a courtesy to the guest in the elevator.

'Which floor, ma'am?' the manager asked politely.

'Eighth please,' she said softly. Her voice was barely audible. He pushed the floor button on her behalf.

She wondered if they could hear her heart exploding inside with every beat. When the elevator stopped on the eighth floor, she stepped out first and stopped to look at her phone as if to check something. The manager and the security representative went past her. Through the corner of her eye, she saw them knock on the door of 805.

'Housekeeping, ma'am,' they announced loudly to the occupant inside. Getting no response, the security officer opened the door with a duplicate key. As soon as the door opened, they saw her body hanging from the fan. The young manager screamed in terror just as the security officer stumbled at the door. In the commotion, Sithara seized the opportunity and ran towards them to catch a glimpse of the ghastly sight. It was devastatingly unreal! Just over two hours ago, they had been conversing normally.

'How could she have committed suicide? This is senseless,' she cried inwardly. Thousands of thoughts and images raced through her mind. She needed a few seconds of normalcy to regain control and stabilise herself emotionally.

A few people had heard the commotion and had rushed into the corridor, catching a glimpse of the disturbing scene. It was dangerous for her to be seen around there. Picking her things from the room was now out of the question, especially in the presence of curious onlookers. She slipped away unnoticed and took the stairs to the lobby. Her heart began to beat again only after she saw Niniya lost in the magazine, seated exactly where she had left her. She suddenly felt a wave of pity for the child. She had just lost her mother. Had it been suicide or had she been deliberately killed? She hurried towards Niniya and said, 'Let's go darling,' Niniya stood up immediately, gathered her things slowly and sauntered towards the lobby exit with Sithara.

Even in those few minutes that she had taken to come

down from the eighth floor by the steps, the news of the suicide of a guest seemed to have reached the front desk as Sithara could see some commotion there. The staff was displaying a range of emotions from fear, shock, grief, curiosity to disbelief. Ironically, for Niniya, the person to whom the tragedy mattered the most, remained calm and blissfully unaware. Her delicate mental health had shielded her from the enormous grief the world had conspired to heap on her family. The two—Sithara and Niniya soon disappeared.

On the way out, Sithara bumped into the same man from the car parking! Suddenly, her body turned stiff with fear. It suddenly struck her that the man bore a striking resemblance to Dr Rangarajan's description of his ISRO assaulter! The late scientist's description fitted the man like a 'T'! He was tall, muscular and tended to lean onto his left side due to a deformity in his leg. Confirming her suspicion further, he involuntarily transferred the car keys from his right hand to the left as she passed him! Fortuitously, Sithara's phone camera was in the perfect place. She captured a full-length image of the man, stealthily, and melted away into the night with Niniya.

WITHIN A couple of hours, the news of Jasmine's suicide reached Tobias Rosenbuch in Germany. He was shattered and was in utter disbelief and filled with grief.

'Where's Niniya?' he screamed at the German consular official who was online from Chennai.

'We've no idea, sir. The police is currently searching for her,' the official reported from ground zero.

'How's that possible? Give me back my baby, my baby…. I can't live without her,' he pleaded, bursting into tears. Hearing his cries, Maren Eysel, Niniya's therapist rushed in, offering support.

A flurry of phone calls were exchanged between India and Germany. A pall of gloom had descended on the Rosenbuch household as the news sunk in. Maren couldn't hold on to the secret that was bothering her, any longer.

'Sir,' she addressed Tobias apprehensively, 'I'm so sorry, I should've told you about this, much earlier, but ma'am prevented me from doing so. The the Indian scientist had passed on some data in the form of a Hindu God to Niniya's iPad on the day he died. I immediately brought it to ma'am's notice,' she paused as Tobias got to his feet menacingly and moved towards her. 'All of this maybe connected with that,' she revealed in fear.

'What are you saying, Maren?' he shouted and hid his face in despair, 'The whole world seems to be after my innocent baby,' he groaned and fell down on the floor amidst loud sobs. 'How will she manage without Jazz?'

'I'm really sorry, sir. Let us pray that nothing will happen to our Niniya,' Maren tried to pacify him. 'But we must at once inform the police,' she reminded him.

Tobias was lifeless and had sunk into an ocean of grief. She took charge and dialled the chief of the German police.

'We have received news just now from the German

Consulate in Chennai that ma'am, I mean, Jasmine Rosenbuch is dead,' she said, absolutely stunned, herself. The revelation was met with a resounding silence.

'Dead? How?'

'They're claiming it was a suicide, but that's totally ridiculous,' Maren said. 'Ma'am wouldn't do a thing like that in a million years.'

'I'm positive, she was murdered,' the chief said emphatically.

'Niniya, where are you?' Tobias cried before losing consciousness.

'Niniya the little girl, who accompanied her mom is missing too,' Maren repeated on the phone to the police chief.

'What?'

'There's something sinister going on, sir. Can you please come here immediately?' Tobias screamed, snatching the phone from Maren. He had regained consciousness and now seemed alert.

'I am on my way,' the chief said, dashing out of the door.

In the police car, he called Vikram who was already at the airport, ready to catch a flight to Delhi. Vikram was waiting to board the aircraft when the call came through. On hearing the news, he cancelled his journey and requested the chief to pick him up on his way to the Rosencuch's residence.

An hour later, they entered Rosenbuch's home together. Maren Eysel briefed them about the Ganesh icon on Niniya's iPad and her theory about the sender.

'I repeatedly asked Ms Rosenbuch if she had any more information or whether the scientist had told her anything. But she never said anything. Now, she's paid the price with her own life,' the chief lamented.

'Do you think they took away my little girl for the same thing?' an agitated Tobias asked. 'The poor kid may not even be knowing what's going on,' he wailed and sobbed.

'Mr Rosenbuch,' Vikram said to Tobias, 'please don't lose heart. I'm saying this with full responsibility that your girl will return home soon. I will promise you that.'

'Thank you, sir, for your very kind words,' Tobias acknowledged wiping his tears. 'My family has nothing to do with your country's politics. Please return my baby, please,' he pleaded as if Vikram had had something to do with her disappearance. Clearly, he was devastated and had lost his ability to think clearly.

'That's exactly the point I'm trying to make, Mr Rosenbuch,' Vikram said feeling sorry for him. 'Your girl is safe and sound. Let's go and get her back. We must leave for Chennai, ASAP.'

'Yes, I must bring her back,' said Tobias as he got ready to leave for India.

'Sir, I'll pack your bag. You stay here,' Maren said, forcing him sit down.

'But… this man said we need to go.'

'Let me also go to India. Niniya will need me and I need her,' she requested the chief.

‘Good idea,’ said the chief. ‘Pack your bag, too.’

‘Alright folks, get ready quickly. Our first stop is the Indian consulate office for emergency Indian visas for both of you. We will proceed straight to the airport from there,’ Vikram said, taking charge.

‘Quick thinking,’ the chief said in appreciation.

‘Meantime, I’ll speak with the Indian ambassador in Germany for his help,’ Vikram said while stepping out. Maren rushed inside.

SITHARA HIRED an autorickshaw and reached her hostel. She had to get organised before leaving the city. From the hostel landline, she called her sister. She told her that Jasmine, the German woman had disappeared under mysterious circumstances, leaving Niniya with her. She did not disclose too many details to her sister, but kept it vague.

‘What are you going to do now?’ her sister asked.

‘I’m going to Indore to sort this thing out.’

‘Why Indore?’

‘Oh! it’s a long story. I’ll fill you in later.’

‘Why are you doing this? That kid is not your responsibility, Sithara.’

‘Whose responsibility is she then? My heart bleeds when I see her left like this. She’s just like any other kid, who should be carefree and happy, doing things that every other girl does, like going to school, then college, get married, have kids of her own. Lead a good life,’ Sithara’s voice drifted away.

'Are you talking about her or yourself?' her sister asked.

A minute's silence followed. 'Both,' she replied, resolutely, and added, 'she's more of me than I actually am.'

'Look, all I'm saying is that this is very dangerous and mysterious. How careless of the mother to leave the kid with you and go away like that,' the sister commented.

'Jasmine was not careless!' Sithara said in her defence. 'I'm there to fight for this kid. Sometimes, I feel I'm born with a self-destruct button. Fate or destiny, keeps me on the move. What remains to be seen is, will I ever get out of this one?'

'Sithara, Sithara,' her sister said in despair.

'Don't worry about me; I'm a survivor and I've work to do, Latha,' Sithara said and hung up abruptly.

She entrusted Niniya to a roommate in the hostel, saying, 'Keep an eye on her, please, I'll be back in half an hour,' she requested.

'Who's she?'

'Huh, my niece, but don't tell anyone,' she said and left before she was asked any more questions.

She returned a while later with food and clothes for Niniya. She fed her sandwiches and changed her into Indian clothes, a skirt and a blouse in sober colors that many young girls wear in Chennai.

'We're going somewhere, dear,' she announced softly to Niniya. She received a blank stare in return. Sithara had a hard time holding back her sobs, but tears flowed down her cheeks. Instantly, she hugged the kid and held her close, and surprisingly, Niniya, let Sithara hold her.

'Who are you? What are you to me? Why do you move me so much?' she questioned mutely. But now Niniya suddenly squirmed in discomfort. She didn't like the physical touch.

'Sorry, sorry,' Sithara apologised to her, letting go of her, at once.

Shortly thereafter, they headed to the Central Station in an autorickshaw. Sithara found seats on a train directly going to Indore from Chennai. At the station, she bought two tickets for travel in an unreserved coach. Tickets for the journey in the reserved sleeper class required a valid photo ID and could possibly pose complications for Niniya, so she thought it wiser to travel with the child in a crowded compartment among the poor and the working class.

Two middle-aged rustic men ogled at her. Sithara avoided eye contact with them. Niniya, tired after a long day, dozed off on her shoulder. As the departure time, came closer, there was commotion with more passengers arriving and trying to squeeze into the compartment. With just a minute or two left for the train to depart, one of the men suddenly swooped down on Niniya and physically lifted her! She cried out aloud.

'Sister,' he shouted over the din to Sithara. 'Come soon, there's a vacant berth in the adjacent coach. You can travel comfortably.'

'I don't want to, please,' screamed Sithara but it was too late. The man who had Niniya had already jumped out and bolted towards the rear end of the train. Sithara ran after him shouting for help from co-passengers, but none came to her rescue. The second man also alighted and ran behind them. Meanwhile, the train rolled out of the platform. After five minutes of frantic chase, they all ended up on a dimly lit, deserted Platform No 16 that was strewn with luggage parcels waiting to be loaded on to a goods train.

'I told you, she would come,' the man holding Niniya laughed maniacally, and bragged to his friend. 'She had no choice.'

The second man said, 'You said first chance for me.'

'Okay, okay go ahead while I warm up with the kid,' the first man said in a north Indian language. He began to molest Niniya, who tried to wriggle out of his grip. 'But make it fast. She looks hot and ready to take both of us at the same time,' they sneered.

'Let her go, please. You can do what you want with me. Please don't harm her,' Sithara pleaded with them.

'I told you she wants it!' the molester said to his friend.

"Then come fast and co-operate, you whore,' the second man said as he pawed her. He squeezed her breasts and tried to undress her. In the melee, he also pocketed Sithara's mobile phone. All the time, Sithara's eyes were on Niniya as she continued to struggle. And then, unaware of the catastrophic repercussions to follow, the first man made a cardinal error! He picked up Niniya's iPad out of curiosity and began fiddling with it. Niniya pull it out of his hand. He slapped her. That was it!

In a jiffy, from a seemingly subdued woman, who was fighting to save herself, Sithara was suddenly transformed into a scorned, ferocious, raging lioness out to destroy her prey! A cylindrical parcel weighing a few kilograms lay on the ground nearby. She picked it up with one hand and smashed it on the head of the man even as he was trying to undress her. It was hit on his head and the blow split his ear. Blood spurted from his wound. He fell back, stunned. Before he knew what had happened, she landed another powerful blow on his jaw. He collapsed to the ground like a sack of rice.

The abrupt reversal of the situation dumbfounded the man who had Niniya. He let go of her. Sithara charged at him with a bloodcurdling cry and went for his throat. He tried to grab her by her hair. At that instant, his forearm was exposed. Sithara savagely bit into it, her teeth piercing his skin. The man let out a yelp of agony. Sithara halted and let out another war cry blood dripping from her mouth. She looked scary and growled like a hungry lion, devouring a tasty meal. The man screamed in sheer terror and dragged himself away from her. She spit blood on him with disgust.

Sithara emerging from her trance-like, possessed state, wiped her face and slowly turned to pick up Niniya. She was in no hurry, now. The first man on the ground squirmed back to life. She kicked hard on his crotch. He rolled over in pain. Sithara took charge of Niniya and holding her by the hand, exited Platform 16 with her head held high. She had ruthlessly brought down two men, double her size! Nothing in the world could possibly stop her now.

She carried Niniya on her shoulders towards the exit, not sure where she was headed. She stopped near a roadside shop and bought a bottle of cold water. She felt better after splashing some of it on her face. She took a swig and gave some to Niniya. An airconditioned luxury intercity sleeper bus stopped nearby.

'Bangalore? I've one berth empty, ma'am,' the conductor said to Sithara.

'Yes, Bangalore, we're coming,' she replied and quietly boarded the bus with Niniya. Anything to get out of this bloody town. After paying the fare, they settled into a comfortable berth. It was then that she realised that her phone was missing. There was nothing she could do about it. She and Niniya fell into a deep and peaceful slumber.

NEXT MORNING, Sithara woke up with a start. Her body felt sore after the pounding she had received during the previous night. It took a while for her to get her bearings right. She noticed Niniya was up already and as usual, was gazing into her iPad.

'Bangalore city is approaching in twenty minutes,' the bus conductor announced. The privacy curtains in between the sleeper berths were drawn back. They could see the other passengers on the bus.

So, what was her next option? Sithara weighed this question. She was supposed to be heading north towards Indore but the ruffians had rudely altered her plans. Yet, she was thankful to God that they had managed to escape unhurt. She must make enquires and think of what to do, she thought. Just then, a co-passenger walked up to her.

'Ma'am,' the man who was dressed in spotless white said to her, 'my name is Krishnan. I belong to the Art of Living Foundation, an international NGO, in the service of humanity. We've our presence in 145 countries.' He handed her his visiting card with a phone number, mail id and complete address.

She studied the card. 'Yes, I've heard of AOL,' Sithara replied humbly. 'In fact, I wanted to join a course some time ago to learn yoga and meditation.'

'You must, ma'am, your life will be transformed,' Krishnan urged her. 'For now, I wanted to talk to you about something else. I've been watching this child for the last ten minutes and have discerned her aura. She has extraordinary potential, a rare glow.'

'Really?' Sithara said, pleasantly surprised.

'Indeed!' Krishnan went on to elaborate. 'I've undergone various training programmes under the spiritual guidance of our beloved Gurudev including *Pranayama,* and *Sudarshan Kriya,* the powerful rhythmic breathing technique. And I can say with authority, that this child is gifted with radiance and positive energy.'

'Thank you so much,' Sithara acknowledged gratefully, like a true parent.

'I suggest you bring her to our International Centre in Kanakpura, not far from the city. We've a meditation and yoga basic course for children of her age starting tomorrow morning. I sincerely think it'll immensely benefit her to overcome her condition,' Krishnan recommended.

It sounded like a wonderful idea, a godsend! Maybe god had wanted this to happen and that's why He had altered their plans! 'When can she join?' Sithara asked.

'Anytime you wish,' he replied with a smile, glad that he could impress her. 'Reach the Ashram at your convenience and call me. I'll meet you at the reception. Our volunteers will help you enroll.'

'Can we stay at the Ashram for the duration of the course?'

'By all means, ma'am,' he said, 'all for a nominal fee that goes towards social welfare causes. You'll enjoy the ashram living experience.'

'Please call me Sithara,' she said extending her hand for a handshake. He graciously joined his hands in a Namaste.

'You and your child are about to blossom like beautiful flowers, Sithara,' Krishnan said, blessing them. She had no reason to tell him that Niniya wasn't her child. It warmed her heart to be called, 'mother'.

On cue, the bus stopped at their final destination and the passengers began to disembark.

'See you soon at the Ashram,' Krishnan said and left.

'Thank you, sir,' Sithara said gathering her belongings. She was the last passenger to get off the bus, while clutching Niniya's hand. The missing sense of direction and purpose were back! Confidently, she proceeded towards a lodge, so that they could both freshen up.

12

The day after the 'alleged' suicide of Jasmine, her husband, Tobias Rosenbuch and Maren Eysel landed in Chennai. Treating it as a special case, the local German Consulate deputed one of the Consulate staff to assist them with whatever they needed in the city. Vikram, the CBI officer had flown along with them up to Delhi. He had to stay back in the capital to report on the progress of the investigation to headquarters. He assured Tobias that he would meet him the next day in Chennai.

Their first stop was the morgue in the government hospital to identify and take charge of Jasmine's mortal remains.

He broke down on seeing his wife in a coffin in the mortuary of an ordinary Indian government hospital. It was a rude shock to the German.

'What have you done, Jazz!' Tobias had wailed aloud, overcome by grief. A part of him had permanently gone dead along with his Jazz. He knew his life wouldn't ever be the same again.

Maren couldn't believe her eyes, either. For her, it all seemed like an extended nightmare and deep down in her subconscious, she was hoping she was asleep and would wake up to find this a bad dream.

Prior to their arrival, it was decided that Jasmine's body would be shifted to Bangalore and cremated in her hometown. The German official in attendance helped look after the formalities. From the morgue, Tobias and Maren were escorted to the police commissioner's office.

'Commissioner,' Tobias spoke in an animated tone, 'this theory that my wife committed suicide is downright outrageous. Ridiculous, if I may add. I know her. You don't, I mean, she wasn't like that at all. She's a fighter and I don't know who's behind this sinister act.'

'Sir,' the commissioner interrupted, 'my condolences for your loss. I know how you must be feeling.'

'No, you don't,' said Tobias as he rose from his chair, in a fit of anger. The German official and Maren had to restrain him. Tobias looked regretful and sat down again. A minute later, he spoke again, this time calmly.

'Look, all I'm asking you is to please find my daughter. We'll just walk away from here. I swear you'll never find me or any member of my family ever in your country for the rest of our lives.'

'Sir, you've to calm down,' the commissioner appealed to him. 'We're doing our best to find your daughter.'

'How on earth do you expect me to be calm, sir?' Tobias demanded, 'my wife has been murdered and the whole damn thing has been made to look like suicide. My daughter is missing. Her fate is unknown. I mean, what's going on in this fucking country?' he exploded.

'Sir, she wasn't murdered. It was suicide,' the commissioner reiterated. 'I will counter you each time you say 'murder'!'

'No, sir, she was,' Tobias cried desperately not having the strength for another slanging match. The other German in the room intervened and said something to him in German. Whatever it was, it seemed to work because Tobias calmed down.

A policeman hurried into the room and whispered something in the commissioner's ear who immediately stiffened. He instinctively picked up his cap lying on the table, put it on and stood up.

'Sir, the honourable Member of Parliament, Mr Senthil, is here to meet us,' he announced and rushed outside to receive him.

A minute later, the MP made a grand entry into the commissioner's office. He stood in front of Tobias and the consular official wondering who among them was the deceased woman's husband. The commissioner pointed to Tobias.

'I'm here on behalf of the government and people of India to offer my sincere condolences, sir,' he said to Tobias while holding his hand. 'It's really unfortunate that she resorted to this extreme step.'

Tobias started to speak and then collapsed in his chair, even as he was being introduced to Senthil.

'Yes, Mr Senntill,' Tobias said, while standing up. 'I've reasons to believe that my wife did not die by her own choice but was killed by someone powerful here, like a politician like you. Oh ,sorry,' he added.

'That's fine,' Senthil retorted in mock jest. 'Politicians are unfairly perceived to be villains.'

'Just like your scientist was done away in Germany by the same people, which, by the way, wasn't an accident.' Tobias elaborated.

'I see. Very strange,' the MP said, while he grimaced and glared at the commissioner.

'Sir, the scientist's case is being handled by the CBI, it's not in our jurisdiction. Secondly, the investigations on the case here have confirmed that ma'am did kill herself,' he said repentantly.

'May I know what are the reasons for your bizarre suspicions?' the MP said, turning to Tobias,

Maren Eysel answered for Tobias, 'The scientist had sent a voice message to Jasmine alerting her just before he died. He had also made a data transfer containing something explosive to her daughter, I mean to her iPad, which we suspect was the prime motive for killing ma'am.'

'And who are you, ma'am?' the MP enquired politely.

'She's with us,' Tobias acknowledged. 'She's my daughter's therapist.'

'Okay, assuming that is true, do you know where's that transferred data now?'

'It's with Niniya,' Maren said.

'And who's Niniya?'

'It's my daughter.'

'Where's she?'

'She's missing,' said Maren wondering if all the politicians in India were so dumb.

The commissioner once again came to the MP's rescue. 'Sir, but we've a problem, there?' he mumbled.

'What?' the MP bawled impatiently.

'Sir, no one has ever seen the little girl,' he said slowly. 'Only they are claiming that the girl came with her mother. We have checked everywhere. There is no sign of her,' he declared regretfully.

'Are you telling me that my daughter doesn't exist?' Tobias thundered, looking at the commissioner in complete disbelief.

Maren and the German official literally jumped in between them.

'Oh my god!' Senthil exclaimed. 'I must sit down,' he murmured, feigning confusion. He, more than anyone else in the room, was acutely aware of the consequences of the so-called data transfer. On the exterior though, he appeared burdened by the complex situation and seemed to be thinking of a possible explanation for this madness.

THAT SAME night, Senthil flew to Mumbai for an urgent one-on-one meeting with Manikrao Kharmate. There wasn't a minute to lose. The situation was turning into a serious threat. From the airport, he drove straight to his party office.

'What's the tearing hurry?' Kharmate asked.

'Your man has evidently screwed up the operation. If we don't clean it up now, we are all going to end up in jail,' Senthil said, firing his opening salvo.

'Jail, really?' Manikrao seemed amused, 'the interesting coincidence is that your fellow Tamilian, that Dr Wrong Rajan also threatened me with exactly the same words.'

'This isn't funny,' Senthil snapped, slighted by the comment.

'I thought so, too. That's why I ordered his killing!' he said without remorse. 'The idiot could've taken my offer of a fortune seriously and saved us all of this shit load of trouble,' he moaned.

'And yet he managed to pass on some incriminating data to that woman to fuck us,' Senthil said.

'How are you sure it is something incriminating? It could also be a bluff,' Manikrao said to Senthil.

'If it was a bluff, why did that woman come here all the way from Germany risking her life?'

'Because she didn't know it was risky?' Manikrao burst into laughter.

'Laugh…laugh as much as you want,' Senthil said sourly, 'Our fate is now in the hands of her mentally retarded kid. And no one knows where she is or what's in that iPad.'

'Look, I'm not breaking my head over this,' Manikrao said, angrily. 'If you've come here only for that, it's your call, entirely. I could've clarified it for you on the phone,' he said coolly. 'It could be a recording of our Delhi farmhouse meeting. So, what? We'll just deny it. And the next time, we will be more careful, unlike that reckless Rohit. I asked him repeatedly if the place was properly sanitised. He assured me it was completely safe.'

'You're missing the main point, Manikraoji,' Senthil warned. 'We've shifted our focus from Diwali Rocket to transfer of data which could be real or fake,' Senthil lamented.

'I think you're overreacting. Who cares about your Diwali Rocket? ISRO as an organisation stands totally discredited today. Meantime, we're nicely milking this murder issue. It's all working to our advantage. Besides, that woman is dead and what harm can a mentally retarded kid who's gone missing possibly do?'

'Manikraoji' Senthil said. 'I've a bad feeling about this whole thing. I suspect someone who knows what is happening has taken the kid.'

'Big deal, so what can we do? Or what do you think, they will do?'

'Extract money in exchange for information, blackmail?' Senthil said.

'Okay, good! So, we'll kill him when he comes to pick up the ransom!' Manikrao said matter-of-factly. 'I think you've been watching too many movies of late. Get real man….'

'Did your man check the hotel room thoroughly?'

'He says he did.'

'But can he be trusted?'

'Of course,' Manikrao thundered. 'He has been my reliable, loyal servant for decades. He would gladly give his life for me. In fact, he reminded me to thank you.'

'Watch out, his types can easily turn against you for money,' Senthil warned.

Manikrao glared at him and said, 'What do you want? What are you implying?'

'Please don't take this personally,' Senthil said, sounding a trifle apologetic. 'Can you call him here?'

'This is unnecessary.'

'I just want to hear from him, firsthand.'

Manikrao summoned Bheekar. He was keen to settle the issue, once and for all.

A few minutes later, the Man Friday strode in confidently but stiffened at the sight of Senthil.

'Good evening, sir,' he murmured.

'Tell him what happened in Chennai,' Manikrao ordered. Bheekar described the murder scene in the sequence it had transpired.

'Did you look properly for the kid?'

'Yes sir, I did,' Bheekar said, still bemoaning the lost opportunity of killing the child. It would've been a glorious first for him.

'But how's that even possible?' Senthil demanded. 'She couldn't have vanished into thin air! The father and the governess told me this evening that the child was inseparable from the mother.'

'I don't know, sir' Bheekar muttered. 'I waited and searched everywhere.'

'Where do you think the half-witted kid is now, Senthil?'

'The kid is with someone. The mother must have sent her out with someone, and that is why she was alone in the hotel room. That's a no-brainer, Manikraoji, obviously they want to cut a deal with people for information,' replied the astute politician.

'Okay, simple!' Manikrao replied. 'Then let's keep an eye open for those people. He has the phone numbers of someone they spoke to.'

'Sir,' Bheekar said in a doubtful voice, 'there's a small problem.'

'What?' Manikrao roared.

'I lost the handbag containing ma'am's phone, my phone, cash, everything in Chennai,' Bheekar confessed.

'What the fuck! How?'

'Jai Maharashtra!' Senthil muttered sarcastically.

'Sir had,' Bheekar revealed, 'arranged logistic support in Chennai like a vehicle, gun, knives, rope etc. After the operation, I had to return all of it to the contact person. When I reached that address, I left it in the car and went first to check on him. By the time I returned, my bag was gone.'

'Never expected that from you,' Manikrao yelled angrily. 'Bloody careless idiot.'

'You should've known that Chintadripet in Chennai is notorious for thefts like that,' Senthil laughed.

'So, what this means is, we are back to square one. Can't follow up on this matter from here,' Senthil summed up, sarcastically.

'But she called someone in Delhi and Indore, sir.'

'We can't be shooting people randomly in the two cities, you creep!' Manikrao said angrily.

'Indore man's initials were PA!' Bheekar recalled from memory.

'Shut the fuck up,' he bawled, 'don't show your ignorance. Allow us to think.'

'Could Rohit be involved in the child's disappearance?' Senthil said, planting another seed of doubt. Kharmate glared at him thoughtfully.

'If that's true,' Kharmate thought aloud, 'then, we've got to get rid of the kid now and the person or persons who are with her.'

'Also, the people they spoke to in Delhi and Indore,' Senthil spelled out grimly.

'God!' Manikrao exclaimed, 'this is becoming a nightmare.'

Bheekar relished the prospect of a growing list of people to be killed but remained silent.

'You keep out of this!' Manikrao barked at him, reading his mind.

'Senthil, can you arrange for a picture of the kid?'

'I brought it with me,' Senthil said gently. He placed a snapshot of Niniya with her flowing golden hair on the table. Both Manikrao and Bheekar came forward and scrutinised it with interest.

THE NEXT day, Manikrao released an official statement to the PTI office in Mumbai after the latest revelations in the investigation of the scientist's death in Germany hogged the headlines in the media.

'The government stands thoroughly exposed in the brutal murder of the Indian scientist. They got him killed because he knew too much. We demand the PM's resignation, and ask for an impartial probe into the sensitive issue. The Parliament cannot function until our demands are met.'

A woman journalist in Delhi managed to catch Rohit Sachdeva's attention at the protest site outside Parliament.

'Sir, reports are coming from Chennai that a woman's body was recovered from a hotel room. She's apparently from Germany. Would you like to comment?'

'I've a lot to comment!' Rohit retorted. 'Right now, only one question—how many more people have to die before the PM opens his mouth?'

'But, sir, the government claims it's a conspiracy to defame them.'

'What are they famous for, I ask? Killing people and creating anarchy?'

'Sir, do you have proof?'

'Does the government have proof that it's a conspiracy?'

The journalist remained quiet.

'I don't need to prove anything, ma'am. People of India are waiting to prove my point. The PM will get a fitting reply very soon,' Rohit said with a charming smile. 'I only ask questions on their behalf.'

'Sir,' the journalist persisted, even while party men at the protest site brusquely pushed her away, 'That's enough!'

JASMINE'S FUNERAL mass was a low-key affair at Bangalore's St. Mark's Cathedral. Apart from her kith and kin, it was attended by most of her friends and acquaintances. Vikram flew in directly from Delhi. Amidst a tearful farewell, Jasmine was laid to rest at the Hosur Road Protestant Cemetery. Ironically, at the same time, Niniya was less than thirty kilometers away at the AOL Ashram. Tobias and Maren briefed Vikram about their meeting with the commissioner of police where Senthil the MP were also present.

'I should've warned you,' Vikram said, 'not to reveal a word about the data transfer and Niniya's iPad to politicians here.'

'We were actually surprised by his visit,' Tobias recalled.

'Now they will also go after her,' he muttered and immediately realised his folly. He did not want Tobias to worry any more than he was already doing. 'Never mind, it doesn't really matter,' he added quickly.

'What are we going to do? Where do we look for her?' Maren asked.

'The embassy has advised me to go to Delhi and seek an appointment with the Union Home Minister of India. I want to make a personal appeal to him to find my daughter. The German Embassy in Delhi is pushing for a meeting through their contacts,' Tobias divulged.

'That's actually a good move, it'll counter any nosey meddling by MPs and State governments with vested interests,' Vikram remarked.

'I had little choice,' Tobias said sorrowfully. 'The commissioner wasn't willing to release Niniya's picture to the media as a missing person! I was ready to offer a million Indian rupees for anyone giving information,' Tobias said. 'Can't understand his problem.'

'Nothing works better in India than through the diplomatic channels,' Vikram told him. 'When orders come from Delhi, no one dares override them.'

'What's your gut feeling, sir, will we find her?' Maren asked, her face marked with worry lines.

'Of course, and very soon,' Vikram assured her emphatically. 'Trust me on this.'

Tobias Rosenbuch closed his eyes in silent prayer.

Not far from where they were, Sithara with Niniya in her lap, pondered over the passage to Indore at the end of the three-day meditation course. The data saga for which Jasmine had laid down her life, had to be taken to a logical end before restoring Niniya to her father. Only then would there be closure.

In the initial days after her mother's sudden disappearance, the kid had withdrawn further into her mute, unfathomable world. She would often squirm and moan in sleep, saying 'Mummy, Daddy…,' alternately. After the commencement of the course, she appeared to be calmer and more receptive. And yet, in Niniya's delicate mind, Sithara, still remained under the category of 'stranger', even though, she did not resist her overtures.

In this rapidly changing situation, Sithara had been pushed into the role of a mother and caregiver. Although she loved the maternal emotions while catering to the child's needs, she was aware that her role was only temporary. The day wasn't far when she would have to part with her. This manifested itself in her mind as a vague fear. There wasn't any doubt that she had grown fond of Niniya, but she knew that her feelings wouldn't ever be reciprocated by Niniya in the traditional sense of the term. She was apprehensive about what would happen in the near future.

13

Sithara and Niniya headed out of the Ashram after obtaining Gurudev's blessings, albeit from a distance as participants in the group. She had arranged for train tickets for Indore with Krishnan's assistance.

'It's our good fortune that we bumped into you on the bus. The last few days have been truly invigorating,' Sithara told him.

'I'm glad you enjoyed your stay here,' Krishnan beamed. 'Often, we tend to ignore ourselves in the rat race of life. Sometimes it is necessary to stop, reflect and introspect. We need to connect the dots that were scattered previously. It helps to find the right solutions to problems and of course in making correct decisions,' he told her, changing her perspective on life.

'Thank you so much,' she said, bowing in gratitude.

'You're welcome; all the best,' he said to them as they parted.

She got a ride to Bangalore City in a fellow participant's car. She thanked him and alighted at the busy Railway Station and proceeded towards the platforms holding Niniya firmly by her hand, much to the discomfiture of the kid.

Upon reaching her second-class sleeper coach, she realised that she had been allotted an upper berth for the journey which was challenging to access with a child. Evidently, all the lower seats and berths were occupied. She was soon to realise that travelling with an autistic child in public had its own set of challenges.

'Sir,' Sithara requested a middle-aged man politely, 'They've allotted me an upper berth for me and my daughter. Can we kindly exchange, please? You know how difficult it is to get up there,' but he wasn't paying attention; his gaze was fixed on Niniya.

'What's wrong with her? Is she possessed or something?' he asked gawking at Niniya's gaze.

Sithara was visibly upset.

The man drew the attention of co-passengers to Niniya. They regarded her with open disdain, unmindful of the fact that they were also scaring the child. Niniya hid behind Sithara.

'Sir, I'm requesting you,' Sithara said snapping her fingers on his face.

'No way!' he retorted. 'She looks like a witch, she is so different. I've never seen such blue eyes … and she doesn't look straight. She can't be from here. We can't travel with such a character,' he declared unequivocally. Some timid copassengers around them seemed to concur with him. A couple of women drew their children closer in fear.

'Don't look in her direction,' a woman reprimanded her curious son.

'We should report this matter to the ticket examiner at once before the train departs,' a man suggested with some urgency.

'If it's necessary, we'll pull the chain and stop the train!' another said.

'She's an autistic child! She won't harm anyone. She's an angel,' Sithara cried aloud but her plea fell on deaf ears.

'Angel my foot! She's a confirmed witch or seems possessed by a ghost.'

Sithara tried to diffuse the situation, but they weren't relenting. A group of disgruntled passengers went to find the TTE. After some serious deliberation, they returned with a railway official, who in turn examined Sithara's ticket and found it to be in order.

'She's a legitimate passenger with a valid ticket,' he informed them. 'I've no authority to ask them to disembark. Everyone mind your own business. Leave them alone.'

There were loud babbles of discontentment.

'I don't want any trouble here. Don't force me to summon a Railway Protection Force constable,' the TTE warned them sternly.

The threat worked. They spoke to each other in hushed tones pointing towards Niniya and henceforth, maintained an arm's distance from her. Sithara emboldened by the official's directive, returned their hostile glare fearlessly. She quietly climbed on to the top berth with Niniya, and ironically found it safe up there. The first night and the following day passed peacefully without further incident. Throughout the journey, though, they were treated as untouchables! None ventured near them, thereafter.

On the second night, Sithara who had dozed off woke up suddenly to find Niniya pursing her lips and eyeing an empty water bottle. The express train was clattering along on the tracks at a furious pace. Sithara knew that if she asked for anything from a co-passenger, it could trigger off a war, so she refrained from asking anyone for water. She gestured to Niniya to stay still as she descended quietly from the top berth, careful not to disturb her co-passengers. It was around 1.15 am.

The TTE was awake and was in his seat. She walked up to him.

'Sir, I need water for my child,' she asked.

'Why don't you...?' he started and recognised the futility of his suggestion. 'I don't have any water, otherwise I would've...,' he said sympathetically.

He looked at his watch and said, 'In another ten minutes, we'll reach Betul station. You may find a shop selling bottled water there,' he told her.

'Okay sir, thank you.'

'You can sit here until we reach Betul,' he said and made space for her. She sat down.

Minutes later, the train pulled into a ghostly, deserted

station. Not a single soul was seen during the scheduled stop for one minute.

'I'm sorry, ma'am,' the TTE said unable to get any assistance for fetching water. After a loud horn from the engine, the train rolled out of Betul and gathered speed again. 'Itarsi is an hour and half away from here. It's a big junction. We'll definitely find shops there.' Just then, they heard a loud thud. Startled, Sithara ran to her berth. Niniya had rolled off the berth and lay sprawled on the floor, dazed by the fall. Her upper lip was cut and was bleeding profusely.

Sithara scooped her off the floor and held her close to her chest. 'It's okay, darling, it's okay. Mamma is here to take care of you,' she mumbled and burst into tears.

Lights came on in the compartment with groans and swear words.

'What the fuck happened?' 'Can't we sleep in peace,' they shouted.

'I told you, we would see blood sooner or later!' one of them said to another annoyed passenger.

'You were right sir, this mother-daughter duo are really weird,' he concluded.

'Quiet,' the TTE intervened like a headmaster trying to control an unruly class. 'The poor child was thirsty. Nothing will happen to you all. Go back to sleep, if you can't help.'

No one came forward to help. Instead, the lights were once again switched off after some more grumbling and cursing.

Niniya cried in agony. The bleeding on her upper lip wouldn't stop despite Sithara's best efforts. She continuously dabbed the wound with a cloth, while the TTE watched helplessly glancing at his watch.

A teaseller had boarded the train at Betul. He saw Niniya's injury and stopped by.

'Sister, put sugar on the wound, it will instantly stop the blood,' he suggested, putting a handful of sugar crystals in her hand. She followed his instructions. The crystals stuck onto the injured part of the lip like glue and miraculously, within minutes, the bleeding stopped!

'If you don't mind, ma'am, she can have water from my bottle,' he offered.

Sithara gratefully accepted and handed over the bottle to Niniya.

'One cannot discount a tea-seller in India, especially around the railways!' the TTE commented.

She ordered a cup of tea from him and drank heartily while Niniya rested on her shoulder.

After the tea seller moved on, the TTE said to her, 'I still feel you must seek medical attention for the child in Itarsi. A qualified doctor should administer a tetanus injection, sterilise the wound, and bandage it. Just as a safety precaution you know.'

How's that possible, sir?'

'I'll endorse your ticket so that you can use it again once you resume your journey. There's a railway hospital in Itarsi close to the station,' he advised.

It sounded like the right thing to do.

'Will it be safe for us at this hour, sir?'

'Of course,' the TTE affirmed. 'You won't be alone. There'll be hundreds of patients in the hospital. Besides, tomorrow morning there'll be plenty of trains for you to proceed to Indore.'

Niniya's upper lip had swollen and turned into a solid black lump.

'Okay sir, I'll do what you say,' she said. Just as the train pulled into Itarsi, Sithara retrieved her bag from the upper berth. The TTE summoned a coolie on the platform and instructed him to guide her and the child to the nearest hospital.

'You'll be fine. God bless you,' the TTE said rather emotionally as Sithara walked behind the man on to an overbridge above the railway tracks and away from his sight.

The coolie at Itarsi station was helpful and guided her to an autorickshaw to the Hospital. The duty doctor, a fresher from Medical College examined Niniya's injury and put a band aid on it.

'She's fine,' he said, 'fortunately the injury isn't deep and should heal in a day or two. The lip is a highly vascular region. I don't want to open the wound. Has she been given her DPT vaccination at age five?'

'I, can't say doctor,' Sithara stammered. 'She's my sister's daughter.'

'Ohh,' the doctor said, sounding surprised. 'Your sister lives abroad?'

'Yes doctor, in Germany.'

'One tetanus injection is recommended just to be on the safe side,' he suggested.

'Sure, go ahead, doctor.'

He administered the injection. The child writhed in pain and cried. Sithara comforted her.

'She'll be fine, nothing to worry,' the Doctor assured her. 'Where are you coming from?'

'Bangalore,' she said, 'actually going to Indore, but this accident on the train forced me to stop here.'

'There's no transport to Indore now, only tomorrow morning,' he told her.

'I'm aware of it,' she said, 'is there any place we can stay until morning, doctor?'

'There's one Hotel Shalimar nearby, barely a five to six-minute walk away.'

'Will I get an autorickshaw, doctor at this time?'

'No need, ma'am,' the doctor emphasised. 'It is very near, just past the Police Chowk,' he said.

A duty nurse rushed in to report an emergency for a patient. The doctor excused himself and followed her.

Carrying Niniya on her shoulders, Sithara walked to the hotel. The road was deserted on this foggy night. Branches of tall trees swayed in the gentle cool breeze, making a spooky noise. Sithara continued walking briskly.

As soon as she turned left, she found a tall, unshaven man with a mean, disheveled look wearing an unbuttoned Khaki shirt, a dirty white vest and loose-fitting trousers blocking her path. He was pointing a double-barreled gun at her, his fingers twitching impatiently on the trigger. He could've been anyone, a dacoit or a bandit from the notorious badlands of Central India or a disgruntled Maoist or even a rogue policeman.

'BROTHER,' SITHARA begged. 'Let us go, my child hasn't had food and is tired. We just want to go to the nearby hotel,' she pleaded. In response, he reversed his gun and leaned forward to smack her. She instinctively, ducked. Fortunately, he didn't carry out the threat.

'If you open your mouth again, I'll kill you both.' It was clear that he meant business.

'Now move,' he nudged her with the cold nozzle pushing at her bare back. She shuddered. Sithara had no option but to follow his command. They walked for about five minutes till they reached a dilapidated house with an open courtyard in front. Reclining on a divan was a tobacco chewing policeman who looked even more frightening than his gun-toting subordinate. His shirt was also unbuttoned and hung loosely over his large, rotund belly. He didn't even look up at them.

'*Maalik*,' the man who had captured Sithara reported, addressing him with reverence, 'this whore was wandering suspiciously near the hospital with the child. She's definitely a child-lifter,' he declared. The master wasn't impressed and did not display any emotion. He grunted and squeezed tobacco in his left palm with the thumb of his right-hand.

They waited patiently for the master's verdict, as the minutes ticked by.

When the tobacco was ready for consumption, he stuffed it into his mouth and also glanced at Sithara for a few, fleeting seconds.

'Where are you from?' he asked her.

'I'm from Chennai,' she said with remarkable composure.

'I was going to…,' Sithara began to plead. He held up his hand to motion her into silence.

On cue, another untidy fellow with a notebook and pen emerged from the shadows. He too took no interest in Sithara's appearance.

'Whose child is this?' the fellow asked while the master chewed on his tobacco.

'It is my child,' Sithara said.

'Where are you going?'

'Indore.'

'What are you doing in Itarsi?'

'My child got injured in the train and needed urgent medical attention.'

'In which train did you come here?'

'Bangalore-Indore Superfast Express.'

'Do you have any papers to prove it?'

What happened next took her by surprise. The master sprang to his feet, slid towards the other fellow and slapped him hard across his face. The sound of the slap reverberated loudly in the quiet night. It made Niniya stir uneasily, while Sithara recoiled in horror.

'Didn't you hear?' the master clarified. 'She has already mentioned that she's from Madras,' he said, referring to the old name for the city. 'People from there are always *pucca* in their documentation. We don't need to verify anything.'

Sithara waited, utterly confused by what was happening.

'There is nothing going to Indore at this hour,' the master said to her, consciously avoiding eye contact.

'In the hospital, they asked me to go to Shalimar hotel,' she muttered.

'*Chutiyas*,' the master cursed the hospital staff. 'We often raid that hotel for whores and pimps. Don't go there,' he cautioned, confirming that they were, indeed, policemen.

'Stay for the night at the Majestic hotel near the Bus Station. It's safe for women.'

'Okay, sir, that is so very kind of you,' she acknowledged gratefully.

'Give her complete protection,' the master commanded, signaling the conclusion of the interview.

'Don't worry, sister,' the master assured her. 'Flag an autorickshaw and see her off,' he commanded his assistant, even as he spat out tobacco and disappeared into the dilapidated structure.

The court reporter proceeded to stick a circular red label on her handbag, 'As long as you're in Madhya Pradesh, you don't need to worry for anything. If anyone confronts you, just show them this sticker. They'll let you go!' he told her.

'What the fuck are you waiting for?' he screamed at the policeman who was now taking it easy. The other two men hurried to help her find transport.

One of them took Sithara's bag and upon reaching the main road, they waited for some form of transport to show up. Just as Sithara wondered how on earth anything could arrive at that hour, they heard the familiar sound of an autorickshaw approaching. Soon a familiar black and yellow three-wheeler appeared out of the white mist. A middle-aged man was driving it. The policeman flagged it down and passed instructions to the driver, 'Take her to the Majestic hotel.'

'And don't take any fare from her. *Saheb's hukum,'* he said conveying tersely that she was being given protection from the cops. He pointed to the red label on her shoulder bag.

The driver seemed to understand and nodded. Sithara caressed the sticker and felt safe. Niniya trotted along beside her, as if half asleep. The policeman gave her a parting salute before the autorickshaw moved forward. Bemused by the show, Sithara sat speechless.

'You're going to Indore, sister?' the autorickshaw driver asked casually. Sithara blinked, resurfacing from her stupor.

'Not now,' she muttered, 'but tomorrow morning. How do you know?' she asked suspiciously.

'That policeman mentioned it!' he replied.

Did he? Sithara jogged her memory of the brief interaction minutes ago. She was positive that the policeman hadn't mentioned Indore! She sat up, suddenly alert. What's going on here, she wondered.

Minutes later, they arrived at the Majestic Hotel. The neon light over the board was partially lit. A man covered from head to toe with a bedsheet was fast asleep on the floor opposite the desk that said, 'Reception' on a small wooden plaque.

The auto driver woke him up. Groaning and cursing under his breath, the 'receptionist' got up, switched on all the lights and took his position behind the desk.

'*Memsahib* needs a room for the night,' the auto driver said on Sithara's behalf.

'We've no rooms for single women at nighttime,' he declared, stating the hotel's policy.

'*Bhenchod!* do you know who she is?' the auto driver said, drawing his attention to the 'red sticker' on her bag.

'Why didn't you say so in the first place?' the receptionist replied and pulled out a ragged registration book from a drawer under the desk. He had a tranquil matter-of-fact response for everything.

'It'll be ₹800 for the night. No room service until after 9 am. No guests allowed. Check out at 12 noon,' he reeled off.

'*Theek hai,*' the auto driver said. 'She'll be leaving this shit hole first thing in the morning.'

Sithara signed on the register and paid the cash in advance. The receptionist led her to their room with a bunch of keys in his hands.

'Good night, sister,' the auto driver said to her, 'I'll take your leave. Buses to Indore leave from here only,' he pointed to the opposite side of the road. 'In case you need anything, I'll be around.'

'No thanks, that will be all,' she said folding her hands in a polite gesture. Latching the door of the room, she collapsed on the bed along with Niniya.

Outside on the road, the auto driver made a call to someone and said, 'She's now secure in the Majestic,' he whispered. The man on the other end sighed in relief.

14

Vikram waited patiently outside his boss's CBI Headquarters office in New Delhi. Soon, he was ushered into the plush chamber.

'Vikram, give me the good news. Are the girl and child on our radar?'

'Yes, sir, they finally are. The special branch officers are monitoring her 24 x 7. As we speak, she's in Itarsi.'

'Thank god!' the top boss exclaimed. 'I don't need more specifics as of now. When we are ready with a plan to deal with her, you can fill me in. She's the last person left in the queue, so we cannot let her out of sight,' he said gazing outside his window. 'But why the hell is she going to Indore?'

'No idea, sir.'

'Is Indore her final destination?'

'We have no further information, sir. Can't speculate,' Vikram stammered.

'She seems tricky to me, Vikram. I'm not getting a good vibe about her,' his boss said deeply suspicious.

'Yes, sir. I came here to clear the air on that aspect. Judging from the information I have, she hasn't done anything devious. Yet….'

The boss gave him a hard glare.

'She appears to be clean. She may have been inadvertently thrust into this orbit of intrigue,' Vikram explained.

'How can you be so sure? She's not a saint. I'm told she has a boyfriend-husband in Germany, a rather unscrupulous fellow. Both might be partners in crime, extracting valuable information from the scientist.'

'That's too far-fetched, sir. She hasn't been in touch with him since the time he left her four months ago. I spoke to her sister. Apparently, the scientist was fond of her.'

'Were they lovers?'

'No sir, not at all.'

'Come on, Vikram,' the boss smirked with sarcasm. 'If not, then why the hell would he pass on national secrets to her?'

'She did not get anything from him directly, sir! Jasmine dragged her into this. And we're still not sure if she's really going to trade national secrets in her possession,' Vikram argued animatedly.

'Okay, calm down,' the boss said, waving his hand.

'Sir, our initial prognosis turned out to be false.'

'Which is?' the boss wanted clarity.

'We assumed she killed Jasmine for the 'data' and kidnapped the child as an insurance.'

'Hmmm, go on, I'm listening.'

'Now we are reasonably sure that Dr Rangarajan and Jasmine were murdered by the same set of men. If she really is part of a team, she would've contacted them by now,' Vikram explained.

'She can still do,' the boss speculated. A minute passed by in awkward silence between them. 'What's her name?'

'Sithara.'

'Quite a charmer she is, it appears,' he remarked. 'Look, in our line of work, we can't be sentimental, Vikram. It makes us weak. We've to strictly follow orders from the top. If they say, get rid of her, we have to, ASAP.'

'Sure, sir.'

'Don't worry, I'll entrust that job to someone else.'

Vikram fidgeted uneasily. 'Sir, with due respect there's nothing personal here, she's a nobody to me,' he stated.

'I know, I know,' the boss acknowledged with a smile. 'I've known you long enough Vikram. In many ways, I respect you for your sense of judgement. I do see your point in this particular case and will bear that in mind.'

'Thank you, sir.'

'Meanwhile, you will be hot on the trail of the girl. I want results. We can't let the girl go out of our sight even for a second. You understand the repercussions, don't you?'

'Yes sir, I do. That train incident where the agents lost her at Itarsi station was unfortunate. It won't happen again,' Vikram assured.

'Hell would've broken loose had they not found her.

There won't be a second chance if a goof up happens again. We'll be forced to kill her, I'm afraid, she'll have to pay with her life for your men's faults! I won't be able to do anything,' the boss said with regret.

'Got it, sir. Things should be clear today once she reaches Indore and we see what she intends to do from there on. Once we're sure of her plan, accomplices, co-conspirators and partners in crime, if any, then we move in,' Vikram said optimistically.

'Good. In case of the slightest doubt, you'll arrest her and wait for my instructions.'

'Understood, sir.'

'There are of course other issues,' the boss grimaced. 'Now the word is out in the open that we have our eyes on her. I must inform you that other government agencies are also watching our backs. Politicians could enter the scene now and try to prevail over the bureaucrats. We've got to protect this girl from them.'

'Okay, sir.'

'Besides the PMO is after me for hourly updates. I've bargained for four days' time. I can't hold them back beyond that.'

'That should do, sir.'

'All right, Vikram,' the boss said. 'Good luck.'

AROUND THE same time as the meeting in the CBI Headquarters, politician Rohit Sachdeva made a call to the

Intelligence Bureau chief, Gurinder Bagga.

'Bagga, oh my Bagga,' Rohit said with a flourish, as if he was greeting and backslapping a long-lost cousin in a family reunion 'How are you?'

Bagga was startled and muttered, 'Sir, sir, I'm fine ji. Thank you so much, sirji'. What can I do for you, sirji?

'*Arre,* work will always be there, *yaar,* but first tell me about Simran *bitiya,* how's she?' he said, fondly enquiring about his daughter.

'She's fine, sirji, she is in her MBBS, final year. Next year, house surgeon then ready for practice by god's grace,' Bagga replied feeling uneasy with the conversation.

'*Sabash*, my child! Very proud of her,' Rohit exclaimed.

'Thanks, sirji, with your blessings, Sirji, how did you remember me today?' He wanted the chat to end quickly. The politician's fake affection for his family was having an adverse effect on the bureaucrat. He was sweating under the collar of his shirt as he sniffed out the undertones in the conversation.

'Alright, if you say so,' Rohit said, adding, 'what's happening in Madhya Pradesh?'

Bagga blinked, 'Which is this one, sirji?'

'Come on, don't fuck with me, Bagga. You know what I'm talking about.'

'No, yes, sirji, I mean which one? What are you referring to, sirji?'

'*Chalo*, I'll give you a clue,' Rohit said playfully. 'Indore!' he whispered. 'Does that ring a bell?'

'*Kya*...Indore?'

'Okay, now let's get serious, no more games,' Rohit said, a hint of hostility in his voice. 'One ISRO woman from Chennai has apparently reached Indore with the German kid. She has in her possession some sensitive information that she's not supposed to have. She's a threat to national security. Time has come for you, Bagga, to repay your loyalty to the motherland, and to me! One man by the name of Bheekar, is already there. Instruct your boys to point her out to him. He'll take care of her. You don't have to do anything. We're doing the 'clean up' act on your department's behalf. You should be happy,' he commanded.

Bagga was both relieved and dismayed—all at once. He believed he would be hauled over hot coals by Rohit and his coterie for the audacity of sending an agent to secretly record an Opposition meeting, at the behest of the government. Presumably, the politician was unaware of this. Not only was he disheartened at the prospect of committing an unethical act of handing over an innocent girl to her killers, he was also left flabbergasted wondering if he would've been better off as a locomotive driver or even as a daily labourer at a construction site carrying cement and bricks on his head! Those seemed to be healthier options!

'Give my love to the family,' Rohit Sachdeva gave a courteous finishing touch to the conversation before hanging up.

Bagga had known all along that the real culprit behind the entire mess he now found himself in, was one of his own agents, Sharad Joshi! He had hated him for the double-cross.

But today, after hearing the politician, he felt proud of his man, 'Serves these bastards right,' he cursed aloud.

SITHARA AND Niniya boarded the bus in Itarsi for Indore around 8 am. Their morning went uneventfully. Mercifully, the swelling on Niniya upper lip had reduced and she was cheerful. A gentle reminder in the morning from Sithara was sufficient for the child to diligently practice a few breathing exercises that she had learnt at the AOL course on meditation and yoga. Sithara was proud of the child. As soon as they settled in their seats for the six-hour ride, Sithara had the uneasy feeling that she was being watched. She reminded herself that she had to be careful. Ever since she had left Chennai, she hadn't had the time to call her sister to keep herself abreast of the developments at ISRO.

A pregnant lady, apparently going back to her mother's home was seated next to her. She began a casual conversation.

'When's the baby expected?' Sithara asked.

'Two months,' the expectant mother revealed with a radiant smile.

'Congratulations!'

'Thanks, is she your daughter?'

'Yes, she's a bit shy in the company of strangers,' Sithara said as Niniya clung to her.

For the next hour or so, the pregnant lady wanted to discuss everything about childbirth and about attending to newborn infants. Sithara explained from whatever knowledge she had acquired over the years, by hearsay. At long last, she made her move.

'Can I make a call from your phone?' she asked.

'Sure,' the lady rummaged for her mobile in her handbag.

'One minute!' Sithara cautioned her, 'there could be thieves on the bus. One should not flaunt your valuables.'

'Oh,' said the pregnant lady, disconcerted by the unexpected warning. She handed the phone over discreetly, along with ear phones.

'Thank you so much,' Sithara acknowledged and dialled Parag Agarwal's number hiding the ear piece beneath her hair. For an onlooker, it appeared as if she was conversing with the lady beside her.

But the call went unanswered. If she's unable to reach Parag Agarwal, she would be badly stuck in an alien town! The way forward for her was only through solving the riddle of the Ganesh icon. Her thoughts were interrupted by the lady again.

'Sister, is it very painful at the time of delivery of the baby?'

'What? No, it isn't. The lady doctor is always there to assist you. Don't worry,' she said to calm her.

'Who was with you?'

'The lady doctor!'

'Only her?'

'Um, my mother was also waiting outside.'

'Oh, okay,' the lady said, 'you're so lucky. Also, you are so kind in letting me know of so many things today, thank you,' she said gratefully.

'You're welcome,' Sithara mumbled.

The phone ringing intruded into their chat.

'I think this is your person calling,' the lady said, gazing at the unknown number on display. Immediately, Sithara answered.

'Who's this?'

'Sir, this is Sithara from Chennai. Remember, Jasmine? I'm her friend.'

'I don't know any Jasmine or anyone from Chennai,' Parag said curtly.

'Sir, I'm Dr Rangarajan's friend. We spoke to you from Chennai. Jasmine and I. You know what happened to her.'

'Heard about that. What do you want?'

Time was running out fast for Sithara.

'I'm in Indore to meet you. It's not been easy for me, sir. You're all big people, well-educated, while I'm just an ordinary woman from a middle-class background. My endeavour is only to salvage the honour of the man for whom I have great respect and regard. I'm not interested in what others think of him. I was told he was your friend too. Wasn't he?'

Silence greeted her.

'Solve the Ganesh riddle for me and I'll never bother you again,' Sithara said, her voice choked with emotion.

'Alright,' Parag said. For Sithara, his consent felt like a monumental triumph. 'Meet me in the parking lot of the Central Museum of Indore at 4 pm.'

'Thank you, sir.'

'If there are any changes, I'll message you later on this number,' Parag added.

'No, no sir. There's no later. This is not my number, no changes, please. 4 pm it will be, please,' she said, hoping that Parag Agarwal would catch the urgency in her voice.

'Okay,' Parag confirmed after a pause.

'Who was that?' the lady asked inquisitively.

'Umm, it's a long story,' Sithara replied.

'Tell me all about it, how else can we kill four more hours to Indore?' the lady said with excitement.

'Actually, my brother works in this man's company,' Sithara wove the story together as the bus chugged along.

AT NOON, the bus pulled into Indore bus station. Sithara helped the pregnant co-passenger, with her luggage and got off the bus. Her parents had come to receive her. She introduced them.

'This is my friend from Itarsi,' she said. 'She's been very kind and took care of me during the journey.'

'Thank you, ma'am,' both the parents said. 'You must visit our home,' the father requested.

'I will, after I finish my work here,' Sithara said, almost instantaneously spotting the gigantic muscular man, Jasmine's killer, scanning the arriving passengers, barely ten feet away from her. She swiftly ducked and hid behind the unloaded luggage from the bus. In doing so, she also noticed two men behind her, who had arrived by the same bus, look in the same direction, wondering what had alarmed her.

Sithara hurriedly took leave of the lady and her family. She ran from the scene trying to take a zig zag route to the exit.

One of the two men following her instinctively clicked a picture of Bheekar and forwarded it to their bosses in the Special Branch with a note saying, 'She panicked when she saw him'. The agents in the Special Branch's IT Cell went on overdrive to identify the man. Within half an hour, his ID had been established. 'He's a politician's hitman. It is clear that she's not involved with them. He's a nuisance on our trail. Keep him away from her,' a terse voice message was relayed to them.

In the meantime, another stroke of extraordinary luck favoured Sithara. She plunged into a shop selling Muslim apparel for woman! She bought a *burqa* and wore it in their makeshift changing room. The silky black robe covered her from head to toe, providing her with the perfect camouflage. She bought a skirt top with a hood and cover for Niniya as well.

Emerging from the shop, she saw the two men who were following her frantically searching for her in the crowd. Sithara nonchalantly walked past them to a restaurant for lunch.

THE CENTRAL Museum of Indore is hardly ever seen swarming with people any more, especially at the time of the year when Sithara was there. In the age of the internet, where information was available to every individual in a single click, few undertook the trouble of going to museums. Learning one's history and looking at the artefacts on display at museums was not a priority anymore. At 4 pm, there were only a handful of visitors. The parking lot was deserted with hardly any vehicles parked there, with the exception of a mini tourist bus. Parag Agarwal couldn't have chosen a better venue for a discreet meeting. He sat in his old vehicle, a Swift Desire parked under the shade of banyan trees and waited.

Still clad in the *burqa,* Sithara emerged from behind a tree and approached him.

'Mr Parag?' she whispered.

'Yes,' he said surprised by a Muslim woman calling him by his name.

She lifted her veil revealing her face, 'Sithara,' she introduced herself.

'Hello,' he said clumsily, 'please get in quickly.'

Sithara opened the rear door and sat Niniya down on the seat, 'I'm right here dear,' she said to her. The child didn't look at Parag and instead peered into her iPad.

Getting into the passenger seat beside him, she said, 'Thank you so much for this.'

For some inexplicable reason, Parag's heart began to race. He felt as if he had just walked into a truckload of trouble.

'Is this a disguise?' he murmured, pointing to her attire.

She nodded. 'People are after me, and I don't know who they are or what they want. I managed to escape, though,' she said casually.

'Oh my god!' Parag exclaimed, scanning the car park. He looked at Niniya who was calm and peaceful.

'Does she know about her mom?'

'No and yes, she can't feel emotions. At least, not outwardly. Maybe she is grieving inside. I don't know. After all this is over, I'll hand her over to her father. Her life too is in danger.'

Parag trembled. She noticed his discomfort.

'Sir, no one knows anything about this meeting,' she said. 'We'll vanish, as soon as our job is done.'

With unsteady hands, Parag opened his laptop and a device to create a WiFi zone.

'Darling, can you type the password which mummy showed you?' Sithara said gently. Her heart pounded while she waited.

Niniya instantly typed 'dR4/L9Gx\RV9W$' and held it up for them to see. Parag's heart skipped a beat. Sithara was shocked.

'How did she do that?'

'I don't know,' Sithara replied wondering how such a thing was possible.

'Now show the Ganesh Icon on your iPad to this uncle. He's a friend of Dr Rangarajan,' she said to Niniya.

She reluctantly loosened her grip on her iPad without looking up. Parag keyed in the WiFi password and transferred the Ganesh icon in no time.

'How does she know Ranga?'

'Don't ask me anything,' Sithara shrugged. He quietly

returned the iPad to Niniya, who in turn was puzzled by the missing Ganesh image.

For the next few minutes, the only sound emanating from his laptop were his fingers clicking on the keyboard and the gentle rustling of leaves in the afternoon breeze.

After what seemed like an eternity, the silence was broken by an indistinct conversation among politicians.

'*Heard ISRO Scientists are patriotic… we'll deal with him… Dr Wrong Rajan.*'

'This is a bloody explosive video,' Parag cried with his hands on his head. 'How did Ranga get hold of this?'

Sithara remained unfazed, 'Will it prove his innocence?'

Parag gaped at her. He wanted to cry out aloud, but he made no sound, realizing the import of this video. His face had turned into a deep red. 'Oh my god, oh my god,' he whispered to himself. 'The Parliament has been jammed because of this. You're going to save a major embarrassment for this government! No wonder politicians are after you.'

Parag was physically present there, but his mind was already racing elsewhere. Sithara placed her hand on his elbow to bring him back to reality. He gaped at her as if she were an alien who had suddenly landed in his car!

'Will it prove that Dr Rangarajan sir is innocent? she repeated.

'Of course!' Parag cried, suddenly feeling uneasy. He began to sweat profusely.

'Sir, will you please calm down and concentrate on the next step?' she told him with a sense of authority.

Parag looked bewildered, asking, 'How can you be so cool?'

He rummaged a pen drive and downloaded the video on to it and handed her the small device.

'Thanks,' she said, as she got ready to leave.

'Look, this video is absolutely priceless,' he said. 'For the country and Ranga's sake, I wish and pray that you deliver it to the right person in Delhi. You must at once leave for Delhi,' he said with a sense of urgency.

'Why can't you keep a copy as a backup?'

He held her gaze, then said steadily, 'I'm not as courageous as you, Sithara. I have a family to support. I don't want this ever traced back to me. Okay, I'm scared,' he confessed and folded his hands in prayer.

She ignored him. 'Niniya, we must leave, darling,' she said to the child.

'Wait!' Parag said. 'How'll you go to Delhi?'

'Train, bus or something. Don't worry, I'll find my way,' she said.

'Please, wait, don't be in such a hurry. I'm unable to keep pace with you,' Parag said to her. 'You must meet Mr Pratap Suri in the PMO! He was very close to Ranga. Karan mentioned his name many times.'

'I've Mr Karan's number; he works in Infosys, right?'

'Yes,' Parag looked dumbfounded. 'How do you know that?'

'From Dr Rangarajan's personal diary!'

'No wonder, Ranga chose you for this job!' he looked

at her with admiration. 'He was always like that, spot on judgement,' he complimented his erstwhile college mate. 'Now, let's see which train leaves for Delhi.'

Meanwhile some visitors had trooped out of the Museum and were walking towards the mini bus. Parag hastened the search on his laptop.

'There's a New Delhi Special leaving Indore in 45 minutes; let's go,' he said and turned on the ignition.

'You're dropping me off at the station?'

'Yes ma'am,' Parag said, 'not only that, I'll book your tickets as well.'

'But you just said you're scared?'

'I was,' Parag said nonchalantly. 'Not any more. I owe it to my friend, Ranga.'

He called a travel agent.

'I want one confirmed berth in the AC Sleeper to New Delhi now. I don't care how much it costs,' he demanded. On the other end, the agent asked for the passenger's name.

'Your name?'

'Saeeda Sharif,' Sithara said without any hesitation.

'What? Okay, age?'

'Twenty-three,' she said. 'My daughter Rubiya is eight years old. Lower berth, if possible, please.'

'Okay, the daughter doesn't require a ticket. Send the mother's ticket to my WhatsApp at once,' Parag said and disconnected.

'Who are you?' he exclaimed with reverence to Sithara.

'A citizen of India, Jai Hind!' she affirmed resolutely.

On the way to the station, he quickly made a hard copy of her confirmed ticket from a computer centre and then drove to the station, dropping her off about fifty meters from the station. 'Okay, you get off here, but I'll keep you in my line of vision from a distance, till the train leaves. I'll call Karan and have him speak to Pratap Suri,' he said.

'Okay, I don't have an ID under Saeeda's name,' Sithara said hesitatingly.

'You'll have to talk your way through that,' Parag said. 'Just in case the TTE demands an ID proof.'

'No problem, I'll handle him,' Sithara said and asked Niniya to get off the car. She took a few steps forward, then returned thoughtfully.

'Do you have sunglasses to spare?'

'What?'

'Simple question, do you have sunglasses?' she repeated.

Parag opened the dashboard of his car and handed over his Rayban sunglasses to her. Sithara put them on Niniya. She didn't make any fuss and appeared to like it as she surveyed the surroundings with her glasses on.

'Shukriya, after we reach Delhi, *inshallah*, I'll make sure they are returned to you. *Khuda Hafis*,' she said, and bade him goodbye, while walking away nonchalantly towards the station, her face veil down.

Parag gaped after her in wonderment, now even more wonderstruck with her guts.

15

As soon as news trickled into the CBI Headquarters about Sithara's disappearance in Indore, Vikram was directed to immediately fly out there to lead the search, find and eliminate the target. He now had clear and unambiguous 'shoot at sight' orders and he issued these to all the agents on the ground. The rider that came along with the order was that the child in her possession should not be harmed in any way and there should be no collateral damage in terms of civilian lives or loss of property. Vikram was met on the tarmac at Indore by his men. They briefed him about the sequence of events at the bus station.

'Thanks to you guys, she's now been elevated to being a threat to national security and is to be hunted down like an animal,' he said ruefully.

'Sir, just for a moment we were distracted. It could've been a planned move by her,' one agent argued.

'Utter nonsense,' Vikram bawled at them. 'You don't know her background. I do. She's smarter than you, that's all.'

The agent wondered why the senior officer from Delhi was supportive of a terror suspect. They drove to the bus station in silence. Upon arrival, Vikram studied the terrain trying to figure out how she could have vanished into thin air.

'She could've gone either this way or that,' he speculated pointing in two directions. 'Find out from those shops in the area if they've seen a woman with a child,' he ordered.

'And summon the conductor of the bus for questioning. Do we have the list of passengers who travelled on the bus from Itarsi?'

'Sir, they don't maintain records of passengers. Tickets are issued on a first-come-first-served basis, based on the number of seats available,' one agent explained.

In the next two hours, they tried to identify and locate the passengers based on eye witness accounts. They hit a dead end. The bus conductor's statement didn't reveal anything either. However, by evening, the shopkeeper who had sold the *burqa* to Sithara gave them invaluable leads. It was a significant development.

Around 10 pm, the CBI chief from Delhi called Vikram. 'Where are you?' he asked with excitement in his voice.

'Sir, we are still making enquiries,' he stated, 'but no concrete leads so far.'

'Don't waste your time there. She's on her way to Delhi by train! Indore – New Delhi Express. She's travelling under the name of Ms Saeeda in A 1 Coach, Berth no 23! And the bigger news is that the PMO says she's a valuable asset to be protected by us!' he divulged.

'What are you saying, sir?' Vikram thought his boss had lost the plot.

'Mr Pratap Suri from the PMO called me. Apparently, the data in her possession is an explosive video in a pen drive that'll put the government in the clear. He wants us to pick her up in Faridabad tomorrow morning at 5.30 am. He's not taking any chances and is coming with us!'

'Why Faridabad?' Vikram asked. 'Why not Delhi?'

'Don't be so naïve, Vikram! Our friends in IB and in the Special Branch have evidently tipped off the politicians. They could be waiting at New Delhi station to bump her off and retrieve the pen drive from her,' the CBI chief explained.

'In that case, why can't we stop the train somewhere earlier?'

'We can, but we don't want to panic everyone on board, especially the girl. We are dealing with a pro here, Vikram. She's smarter than we imagined. For all we know, if she's alive at the end of it all, she might be the next CBI chief! Seriously, the only problem is, she could end up with the very people who are out to kill her! She doesn't know that we are the ones trying to protect her,' he said.

Vikram's mind was busy thinking of various possibilities.

'What the hell are you thinking, Vikram? We've no time to lose,' the CBI chief literally screamed.

'Sir,' Vikram yelped loudly.

'Get back to Delhi in the next three to four hours. I don't

care how you reach! We're leaving for Faridabad with the PMO official at 2.30 am,' he ordered.

'And tell your boys to put the guns back in their holsters. If anything happens to the girl, god forbid, I'll personally shoot them all,' the chief warned ominously and disconnected.

'BHEEKAR IS missing since yesterday,' Manikrao Kharmate said to Senthil.

'At this critical hour?' Senthil sighed, 'I never trusted him. I don't trust Rohit either,' he said.

'There are no permanent friends or foes in politics,' Kharmate said. 'Don't know where this idiot went. It is unusual though. I think something must've happened to him.'

'But there must be others to do the job?'

'Plenty,' Manikrao said with a crooked smile. 'That bitch is not coming out of New Delhi station alive,' he said determinedly.

'There will be a thousand passengers on the train. How'll we locate her?'

'Rohit's IB contact gave the coach and berth number, A1 Berth 23.'

'Wow, that's easy now,' Senthil said, sounding happy. 'But please caution your men, there could be Special Branch men also in mufti. We can't afford another failure.'

'It's all under control this time,' Manikrao said, brimming with confidence.

OVERNIGHT, INDIAN Railways upgraded train number *12415* from Indore to New Delhi to Top Priority status. Security was enhanced in all stations along the route. No unscheduled stops were to be made whatsoever for any reason, the railway staff on duty were informed. All eyes were focused on the train.

It was a well-known fact that the Union Railway Minister of India often slipped out of his official residence in disguise and travelled incognito on random routes to make an on-the-spot assessment of passenger problems. Taking advantage of that, a rumour was deliberately spread among railway staff.

They were told that the minister was on a secret trip in the night and unfortunately his ID had been compromised. It has become a security issue, they were told.

At 5.30 am on the following morning, as per plans, Pratap Suri entered the AC Sleeper Coach A1, at Faridabad station as soon as the train came to a halt. Vikram was right behind him. Sithara was awake, but lying down lost in her thoughts.

'Good morning, Sithara dear,' Suri greeted her softly after introducing himself. He showed her his ID badge dangling from his neck with bright red letters that said, 'PMO'. Vikram kept a close watch on her. Taken by complete surprise, she gawked at them.

'It's okay, dear, there's no need to panic. I was told you were coming to Delhi to meet me so I thought I'll surprise you here. I hope you don't mind,' Suri said with a disarming smile.

Sithara uncertain about this sudden development, remained quiet and unmoved.

'Dr Rangarajan, your mentor, was a good friend of mine,' Suri said producing a picture that had both of them smiling. He gently handed it to her making sure there were no hasty movements.

'I'm sorry you have had to go through lots of hardship to reach here, dear. But, let me tell you, we are all very proud of you. Dr *Saab,* wherever he is, must be very pleased,' Suri said, when suddenly Sithara held his hands and broke down. Her reaction, eased the tension in the air.

'It's okay, dear. Cry aloud if it makes you feel better,' Suri encouraged her placing a hand on her head like a father. Sithara, took her time, eventually composing herself. Suri and Vikram waited patiently. She wiped her tears and opened her handbag. Instinctively, Vikram's hand closed in on the gun. She retrieved the pen drive and put it in Suri's hand, saying, 'This is your property, sir'. There was substantial relief on her face.

'Dr Rangarajan was a good man,' she said.

'I know, dear. And you're the best. Thank you for this,' he said depositing the pen drive in his pocket. 'We are holding up this train. We must get off soon, otherwise the passengers on board are going to curse us,' he said, smiling.

Sithara helped Niniya to get up. Vikram helped her retrieve her bag. They got off the train and walked out of the platform surrounded by gun-toting commandoes. Behind them, ever so slowly, the train rolled out of the platform towards Delhi.

'You gave us quite a run for our money,' Vikram remarked to Sithara shaking his head. Pratap Suri found it highly amusing and laughed aloud.

FORTY MINUTES later, the special express train came to a halt at the New Delhi Railway Station. Some mean-looking assailants dressed as coolies and railway cleaning staff but armed with guns surrounded the exits of the A1 Coach as the passengers disembarked, one by one. Not finding the persons they were looking for, they rushed to Berth no 23. A passenger seemed to be asleep with a bed sheet cover over him. One of them threw the bed sheet away. There was no human underneath, only skilfully arranged spongy pillows. On top of one of the pillows was a white sheet of paper with an exquisitely drawn image of a hand, prominently showing the middle finger pointing upwards! Just in case, the intended message of the image was lost on the reader, written neatly across were two words in English, '*Fuck you.*'

16

It was a beautiful spring morning in Delhi. The days of winter smog and polluted air quality had lifted to give way to clean, fresh air and mild weather. Manikrao Kharmate sat in his guesthouse wondering about the uncertain future ahead. The mysterious woman had hoodwinked them all. He spoke to the IB chief, who too seemed clueless about her identity and whereabouts. Out of the blue, his mobile phone vibrated. A call from a private number!

'Hmmm,' he said rather carelessly.

'How much are you willing to part with for the pen drive?' a woman's voice asked.

'Who's this?'

'How does it matter? Did your boys like the message I left in the train?' she said, sounding smug.

'Oh! How did you get this number?'

'Why? Are you already on the Interpol's lookout list? That will make it difficult for me to reach you! Aren't you the leader of a political party representing people like me?'

'I think we underestimated you,' Manikrao muttered mournfully.

'Look, that's your problem. You are wasting my time. Well, if you're not interested, fine. There are others in the market. Your Delhi friend for instance,' Sithara's voice had a swag that invariably followed a triumphant success.

'Really? And you think you can get away with this?' he said as he tried to match up to her cockiness.

Immediately, a request came to turn the audio into a video call!

'Accept, if you've the balls, Manikrao,' Sithara challenged him.

More out of anger and a badly bruised ego, he accepted. On his screen, he saw the image of a Muslim woman in a *burqa* with the veil slowly drawn up revealing her face. She had on a pair of large sunglasses.

'I know this isn't a big deal for you. I also know that politicians of my beloved country, come with the thickest skins and the thinnest morals. Seldom do they get convicted. But, this,' she said, holding up the pen drive, 'this round you've lost and I've won,' she said.

'When you called on my personal number, I knew.'

'I wanted to have some fun. Curious to see how a loser looks!'

'I'll get to you one day, bitch. How long can you hide?'

'Come on, don't be a sour loser. You're ruining the moment for me!'

'How dare you? Do you realise with whom you're talking?'

'Go to hell,' she whispered and waved him a cocky goodbye.

He disconnected the call and threw his phone away.

An hour later, the secretly recorded video tape of the Opposition meeting in a farmhouse was telecast on all news channels with blaring headlines: 'Breaking News,' 'Biggest Expose of the Year' 'Leaders Plotted to Kill Indian Scientist'. Pictures of hitman Bheekar in CBI custody, who had turned approver were also flashed on the screen.

Journalists with OB vans camped outside the official residences of Manikrao Kharmate and Rohit Sachdeva for their reactions. The ruling party's spokesperson was at her combative best and full of moral indignation at the emergency 'Press Meet' explaining the plot and demanding answers. She asked for resignations and accountability from the Opposition, blasting them!

Meanwhile, Niniya was safely handed back to her father. It was rare for her to show emotions, but this time, Niniya jumped into his outstretched arms as soon as she saw him. Tobias and Maren thanked Sithara profusely. They invited her to Germany to be with the child. Sithara kissed Niniya goodbye and as a parting gift, the little girl showed her iPad, wherein Sithara's name and picture were keyed in as 'Ma'. She broke down and held Niniya tightly and muttered, 'I'll miss you, darling.'

By the afternoon, Rohit Sachdeva on behalf of the Opposition, issued a statement.

This is a complete lie. We deny any involvement. The video tape is outright fake. Its authenticity needs to be verified by a competent forum. The so-called expose is nothing but treachery and fraud to defame the Opposition because the government does not have answers for the issues raised against the Prime Minister. Only an impartial probe in this case will bring out the truth. Our agitation will continue until then.

ISRO released a statement imposing a life ban on the MP, Senthil, barring him from entering their Space Centre or any of their offices in India and abroad.

A high-level probe was ordered into his specific role in the murders of Dr Rangarajan and Ms Jasmine Rosenbuch.

MISSION ANTARIKSH

Wednesday, 27 March 2019

India's Prime Minister made a special announcement interrupting a scheduled news bulletins at noon – India had successfully tested the country's first space weapon, an anti-satellite missile. India became the fourth country to acquire the ability to shoot down satellites, after America, Russia and China.

'Our scientists have hit a live satellite 300 Km away in low-Earth orbit. The indigenously produced interceptor is a major step forward for the country's national security. The weapon gives the country the ability to destroy an enemy's satellites, potentially disrupting capabilities in agriculture, defense, navigation and communications although it has never been used in combat. Let me reiterate that India has no intention of entering into an arms race in outer space. We've always maintained that space must be used for peaceful purposes only. I dedicate the success of '*Mission Antariksh*' to Dr Rangarajan's memory,' he proudly added.

PRATAP SURI handed his phone to Sithara: 'PM is on the line' he said to her.

'Hello Sithara *beti*, how are you doing?' he greeted her with fatherly love.

'Sir, sir I'm fine. Thank you, sir, I'm so overwhelmed by this call and I don't know what to say,' she said in excitement.

'Not at all *beti*, what you've done is nothing short of a miracle. I must be the one thanking you. You've saved my government. If there's anything I can do for you, please let me know,' he asked.

'Sir, I need a job,' Sithara asked without hesitation.

'Haven't they informed you?' There was a pause for a few seconds and the PM spoke again, 'You're appointed by the Union of India to work as an undercover Special Agent for the CBI! The country needs girls like you. Congratulations, god bless you, *beti*,' he said.

Epilogue

People of India's response to the PM's announcement of acquiring a 'Space Weapon' was negligible. It did not gain any traction for the ruling party, coming as it did, weeks after the country had exchanged tit-for-tat airstrikes with its neighbour. No one was bothered. The Opposition leaders while congratulating Indian scientists wished the PM a happy World Theatre Day! Nonetheless, the PM and his government won handsomely in the general elections that followed, and began their second term with a flourish.

Acknowledgements

My sincere gratitude to the respected Sri Chetan Mahajan for inviting me to his spectacular writing abode – the Himalayan Writing Retreat – which serves as a magnificent inspiration for aspiring authors like me. The core idea for this novel took shape in the heavenly HWR in Chetan's presence. Thank you, Sir, for the invitation and your hospitality. I'm also indebted to the sprightly Dr K P Naveen, Professor at IIT Tirupati for his inputs during the time spent with me. His impetus hastened the entire writing process. A special mention to my daughter Sivani and son-in-law Abhishek for driving me to several places in Germany, which serves as a backdrop for the novel.

Finally, my grateful thanks to the 'Literary Agent', Sri Suhail Mathur of The Book Bakers, whose tireless efforts facilitated my introduction to Ms Renu Kaul of Vitasta Publications, the publisher of this novel. With Suhail and Renu on board, I was sure from day one that I was in safe hands and that the journey of this novel would be complete.